W9-CQP-847

"Chantal, has it occurred to you that I am attracted to you for very basic, honest reasons? Because I think you're beautiful? Because you're unique and there's an aura of mystery surrounding you that I find incredibly sexy?" Scout said.

He reached across the table and took her hand in his. "I haven't wanted to kiss you since the minute I laid eyes on you because of, or in spite of, who your parents are, but because you have one of the most enticing mouths I've ever seen. You've got skin that feels like a flower petal, hair dark as midnight, and eyes like bottomless lagoons. Chantal, I want you as I've never wanted a woman."

Slowly she released the breath she'd been holding for so long she couldn't remember the last time she'd exhaled. "You shouldn't say things like that to me, Scout."

"Why not? I want you to know how I feel, to know why I desire you. Why won't you believe me?"

She pulled her hand from his, stared at the imprint his fingers had left on hers, then looked into his dark eyes. "Because of your fiancée . . ."

WHAT ARE *LOVESWEPT* ROMANCES?

They are stories of true romance and touching emotion. We believe those two very important ingredients are constants in our highly sensual and very believable stories in the *LOVESWEPT* line. Our goal is to give you, the reader, stories of consistently high quality that may sometimes make you laugh, sometimes make you cry, but are always fresh and creative and contain many delightful surprises within their pages.

Most romance fans read an enormous number of books. Those they truly love, they keep. Others may be traded with friends and soon forgotten. We hope that each *LOVESWEPT* romance will be a treasure—a "keeper." We will always try to publish

LOVE STORIES YOU'LL NEVER FORGET
BY AUTHORS YOU'LL ALWAYS REMEMBER

The Editors

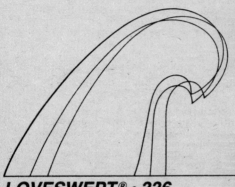

LOVESWEPT® • 336

Sandra Brown

Temperatures Rising

BANTAM BOOKS
NEW YORK • TORONTO • LONDON • SYDNEY • AUCKLAND

TEMPERATURES RISING

A Bantam Book / July 1989

LOVESWEPT® and the wave device are registered
trademarks of Bantam Books, a division of
Bantam Doubleday Dell Publishing Group, Inc.
Registered in U.S. Patent
and Trademark Office and elsewhere.

All rights reserved.
Copyright © 1989 by Sandra Brown.
Cover art copyright © 1989 by Susan Tang.
*No part of this book may be reproduced or transmitted
in any form or by any means, electronic or mechanical,
including photocopying, recording, or by any information
storage and retrieval system, without permission in
writing from the publisher.*
For information address: Bantam Books.

*If you would be interested in receiving protective vinyl
covers for your Loveswept books, please write to this address
for information:*

Loveswept
Bantam Books
P.O. Box 985
Hicksville, NY 11802

ISBN 0-553-22001-2

Published simultaneously in the United States and Canada

Bantam Books are published by Bantam Books, a division
of Bantam Doubleday Dell Publishing Group, Inc. Its trademark, consisting of the words "Bantam Books" and the
portrayal of a rooster, is Registered in U.S. Patent and
Trademark Office and in other countries. Marca Registrada.
Bantam Books, 666 Fifth Avenue, New York, New York 10103.

PRINTED IN THE UNITED STATES OF AMERICA

O   0 9 8 7 6 5 4 3 2 1

One

Sloe-eyed. Sleek hair. Slender figure.

Scout Ritland mentally summed up his first impressions of the woman he spotted across the ballroom. She was a stunner, a definite standout.

Between the two of them milled a crowd of black-tie-clad celebrants getting drunk on self-congratulations and a tropical fruit punch that made even the stuffiest imbiber feel loose enough to skip naked through the Pacific surf.

Scout wasn't quite that far gone, but he was experiencing a pleasant buzz. It was as loud as the calls of the night birds in the jungle surrounding the landscaped grounds of the Coral Reef, the spectacular resort that was enjoying its official grand opening tonight.

The potent punch had a tendency to thaw inhibitions, suppress morals, and vanquish previously held ideals pertaining to sexual equality. Eyes glazed by intemperance and uncharacteristic chauvinism, Scout stared at the woman in the clinging white dress. Without a smidgen of remorse he was assessing her only as a sex object.

Parrish Island had that effect on people. The place, no more than a dot in a chain of dots on a map of the South Pacific, was intoxicating. Fragrant flowers, banyan trees, and coconut palms abounded; Yankee pomposity did not.

Only a few hours earlier Scout had finally succumbed to the island's allure. For the first time since his arrival months before, he had looked beyond the shell-pink-marble walls of the hotel. Up till now it had consumed so much of his time, energy, and thought, he hadn't had an opportunity to enjoy the unspoiled island and its friendly inhabitants.

One inhabitant in particular—the woman in white. Damn, she was gorgeous. Aloof. Even a trifle haughty. She had noticed his stare and had returned it with a cool appraisal of her own. Then, as though nothing about him could possibly interest her, she had studiously ignored him ever since.

Scout was intrigued. He hadn't seen her around the resort while it was still under construction, so she wasn't a hotel employee. The wife of an employee?

That was a hell of a dismal thought. He discarded it along with his recently emptied glass. If she was married, where was her husband? What guy in his right mind would let a woman who looked like her run around loose in a room full of men who had been separated from hearth and home for months?

No, Scout doubted she was married or seriously attached. She didn't have a "taken" look about her. Then who was she, he wondered as he disinterestedly surveyed the array of exotic foods on one of the buffet tables while keeping her in sight.

"Great job, Mr. Ritland," someone commented in passing.

"Thanks."

A large portion of the resort hotel was built out over the waters of a placid lagoon. Scout had engineered the marvel, working together with the architect. Because of his ingenious efforts, he was receiving his share of the glory. His hand had been shaken so many times, it was cramping. His shoulder was sore where it had been heartily slapped in congratulations for a job well done.

Reeling with the inebriation more of success than of the fruit punch, he wended his way through the crowd. His destination was the woman standing beneath one of the high, arched openings leading outside.

When he got within speaking distance, she turned suddenly and looked directly at him. Scout was stopped dead in his tracks. He sucked in a quick breath.

The almond-shaped eyes, tilted up slightly at the corners, weren't dark brown as he had expected, but blue. Neon blue. Electrifying and stupefying blue.

"Scout, where are you off to? Glad I caught you before you got away."

His elbow was grabbed from behind and he was brought around. Keeping his gaze locked with the woman's for as long as possible, his head reluctantly followed his body around. "Ah, Mr. Reynolds." He shook the hand extended to him.

"Corey," the hotel magnate corrected Scout. "You've done a terrific job. Getting tired of hearing that yet?"

Scout shook his head and laughed self-derisively. "Never."

"It goes without saying how pleased we are. I speak for everyone in the corporation."

"Thank you, sir." Scout couldn't afford to be rude to the man who had signed his hefty paychecks, but he glanced quickly over his shoulder. She had disappeared. Damn!

"It wasn't an easy undertaking," Corey Reynolds

●

was saying. "Especially when one considers all the hardships you faced during the construction."

Scout asked, "You mean the islanders' attitude toward work?" The other man nodded. "They definitely do not comprehend the meaning of deadlines or the eight-hour workday," Scout said ruefully. "Overtime incentives never lured them away from a celebration, and they have about ten of those a month. That didn't bother me nearly as much as the thievery, though. I apologize again for going over budget on the supplies."

"It wasn't your fault that they kept disappearing. I know you tried every way you could think of to catch the thieves."

"Wily bastards," Scout said beneath his breath. "I even sat up four nights straight keeping vigil. The night I decided that it was futile and went to bed, we were hit again."

Catching a glimpse of white out the corner of his eye, Scout swiveled his head toward the terrace. There was nothing there but moonlight and sultry, fragrant air. Was she still out there, lurking in the shadows of the tropical gardens?

". . . with yourself?"

"Huh?" What had Mr. Reynolds asked him? Oh, yes. "No, I haven't seen anything of the island except the area immediately around here. I thought I'd take off a week or so before flying home."

"Good idea. Give yourself time to wind down before your wedding. I presume it's still on."

"Late next month."

Mr. Reynolds smiled and asked, "How is Miss Colfax?"

Corey Reynolds had been introduced to Jennifer Colfax at a dinner party in Boston, where the Reynolds Group was headquartered. At that point the Coral Reef resort had been only an architectural rendering. It pleased Scout that the CEO remembered his fiancée's name. He could always count on Jennifer to make a good impression.

"Her letters indicate that she's fine," he replied.

"Still beautiful?"

Scout grinned expansively. "Very."

The older man chuckled. "You're a trusting young man to leave her for this long a time."

"We came to an understanding before I left. I couldn't very well expect her to sit home alone every night while I was away. She's been free to date, as long as it's kept on a platonic basis."

"You're not only trustful, but generous. Still, I know she's eager to have her fiancé back in the States."

Scout shrugged. "She went to Europe for several weeks during the summer. And she's had her aunt's antique shop to help keep her busy."

"Oh?" Reynolds inquired with polite interest. "What does she do there?"

"*Dabbles* is the word that comes to mind." Jennifer did a lot of dabbling—in antiques, in music, in fashion.

"My wife dabbles too. When she's not shopping," Corey Reynolds added on a laugh. Sipping at his glass of punch, he asked, "Lovely, aren't they?"

Scout followed the direction of Mr. Reynolds's gaze. He was watching one of the island girls hired for the night to serve canapes. She was dressed in a short floral-print sarong that had been artfully wrapped around her lithe body. Like most of the island women, she was petite and very pretty, with glossy black hair, snapping dark eyes, and a ready smile.

"Even though I'm engaged to be married," Scout said, "I haven't failed to notice that one of Parrish Island's natural resources is its lovely female population."

Reynolds directed his attention back to Scout. "What do you plan to do here on the island during your R and R?"

"Lose myself. Escape from delays, slow-moving workers, and the telephone. Go fishing. Maybe get in some hunting. Body-surf. Lie on the beach and do absolutely nothing." He leaned forward and added, "If I get captured by a lovely, bare-breasted native girl, don't come looking for me anytime soon."

Corey Reynolds chuckled and slapped him on the back. "You rascal. I like your sense of humor." They shook hands and, again, Corey Reynolds praised Scout's engineering feat. "I'll see you back in Boston. I want to talk over some future projects with you. Let's you, the lovely Jennifer, and I have lunch soon."

"We would enjoy that very much, sir. Thank you."

Watching the older man move away, Scout was barely able to contain his excitement. He didn't want to become part of the Reynolds Group. His personality didn't fit the corporate mode. He would find that environment creatively stifling. But he certainly wanted another contract with the Group, and it looked as though that was what Corey Reynolds had in mind.

The Coral Reef resort project had been Scout's first break into the big time. He knew the importance of capitalizing on his success while he was still on the minds of the decision makers.

After his talk with Corey Reynolds, he felt even more that he had something to celebrate. Taking another glass of punch from a waitress bearing a silver tray, he moved through the archway to the terrace beyond.

The exterior walls of the sprawling resort were garnished with bougainvillea vines heavy with clusters of their vibrant flowers. No expense had been spared to decorate the hotel inside and out. Priceless Oriental urns held lush ferns and ornamental palms. Natural plumeria trees had been pruned to perfection. Like gigantic fireflies, torches flickered inside stonework lanterns, strategically placed along winding paths through the gardens.

From the main terrace, wide, shallow steps led down to another level. One path curved left toward the trilevel swimming pool with its manmade waterfall and ornate fountains. Another path led down to the beach, where the sand was a pale blond ribbon between the manicured lawn and the gently lapping surf.

Revelers seeking privacy had drifted out of the ballroom. A group of Asian men discussed business over drinks at a table on the lower terrace. Beneath a palm tree on the lawn a couple kissed, oblivious to everything except each other. Another couple strolled hand-in-hand in the surf, still wearing their evening clothes, their shoes dangling from their hands.

In the center of the moonlit panorama stood a solitary figure. Scout, as one under the command of a hypnotist, moved down the steps toward her. The moonlight on her white dress made her as visible in the darkness as the beacon of a lighthouse. She stood motionless, facing the ocean, staring across the water as though communing with it in a silent and sacred manner.

Helluva dress, Scout thought as he moved closer. Jennifer wouldn't have approved of it. Not many New England women would have. It was painfully simple but blatantly sexy. There was a high slit on one thigh. One shoulder was left completely bare by the form-fitting garment. The balmy breeze molded its fabric to her, delineating her breasts and the V of her thighs.

Scout's thoughts were the same ones that kept priests in business.

He felt a momentary stab of guilt because of Jennifer. But she was on the other side of the world. This island seemed as far removed from Jennifer and Boston as another planet. Rules and codes of behavior that applied there were of no more use here than a woolen overcoat.

He'd been working nonstop for months. He'd earned one night of pleasure, hadn't he? He had been living in one of the most exotic spots on earth and hadn't had a single chance to sample its pleasures.

The rationalizations marched in file through his brain, but even without them he would have acted. Months of sexual abstinence, the potent liquor he'd drunk, the tropical setting, the beautiful woman, were a powerful combination of aphrodisiacs he couldn't resist.

Hearing his approach, she turned her head and gave him another piercing stare with those breathtaking blue eyes. Hair darker than midnight had been pulled back into a low bun on her nape and decorated with two white hibiscus blossoms. Her only jewelry was a pair of single pearl earrings, each pearl as large as a marble.

As flawless as they were, their opalescence was no competition for her skin. It was creamy, smooth, incredibly flawless. There was a lot of it showing too. Neck. Chest. The curve of one breast. Legs. She wasn't wearing stockings with the high-heel sandals. Even her feet were pretty. So were her hands. In one she carried a small satin evening bag.

Such loveliness, such rarity, such perfection. Scout's body was pulsing with lust.

She was standing beside a piece of sculpture. It represented a pagan god who was wearing a puckish grin and sporting an exaggerated phallus. Scout remembered the day they'd set the statue in place. It had been the talk of the work site. There'd been a round of jokes made, each more lewd than the preceding one.

Now he could swear the statue's insolent grin was aimed at him. It was as if the little devil knew about his physical condition and was maliciously delighted. He nodded at the idol and spoke to the woman.

"Friend of yours?"

He was hoping for the best, but halfway expected her to rebuff him. His heart expanded when her lips, glossy and tinted, parted in a smile that revealed teeth as flawless as everything else.

"He's everybody's friend. He's a god of eroticism."

Ah, good. Language wouldn't be a barrier. She spoke English. It was accented, but beautifully so. Her voice was low and husky, with the whisper of the surf behind it.

Scout smiled wryly. "I could have guessed that. What's his name?"

She told him. He frowned. "That has at least twelve syllables and they're all vowels." Since his arrival, he'd mastered a few words of the native dialect, but they all had to do with construction. "Get back to work" was hardly what he wanted to say to this woman.

But even if he'd known the correct words, he couldn't say what was on his mind. *This little guy has nothing on me in the arousal department. I'm hard as a rock, and, baby, you're the reason. Your place or mine?* Those words hardly seemed appropriate for opening a conversation.

"My name's Scout Ritland." He extended his hand.

She gave him hers. It was cool and small and soft. "Chantal duPont." Withdrawing her hand, she added, "It was a pleasure to meet you, Mr. Ritland," and turned to go.

It took a moment for Scout to recover from her dazzling smile and the feel of her hand in his. When he did, he fell into step alongside her as she took one of the shell-gravel paths toward the perimeter of the resort's property.

"Will you be working at the hotel?" he asked in an effort to prolong their brief conversation.

She shot him an amused glance. "Hardly, Mr. Ritland."

"Then what were you doing at the party?"

"I was invited."

He was forced to catch her arm in order to detain her. She came around to face him. The moon cast intriguing shadows over her face through the overhead trees. "I didn't mean to sound rude," he explained. "Of course you were invited. It's just that I haven't seen you around, and I wondered what—"

"I didn't take offense," she interrupted softly.

He stared down at her, captivated by her exquisite face, her eyes, her mouth. His fingers were still around her upper arm. He'd never felt softer skin. Her eyes moved down and pointedly called attention to the fact that he was still touching her.

Regrettably, he relaxed his hold. Only when he dropped that hand to his side did he realize that in his other, he was still carrying the glass of punch.

"Care for a drink?" he asked, feeling a little ridiculous.

"No, thank you."

"Can't say that I blame you. It's stronger than a swift kick from a mule."

Giving him a ghost of a smile, she reached for the glass and brought it to her lips. Watching him over the rim, she drained it, then ran her tongue over her lips, licking up every drop. "Unless you've cultivated a tolerance for it, Mr. Ritland." She passed him the empty glass and stepped off the path, entering the jungle.

Scout stared after her, amazed. That much liquor,

imbibed that quickly, would have knocked most grown men flat on their backs. She'd swallowed it like mother's milk and was still standing. Not only that, she was negotiating the dark jungle path as silently and expertly as a nocturnal predator. Leaves barely stirred with her passage. No sooner had he formed that thought than she slipped through a screen of vines and disappeared.

He dropped the glass on the overgrown path and charged after her, thrashing his way through dense foliage, mindless of his tuxedo. An insect whizzed past his ear like a missile; he swatted at it heedlessly.

"Chantal?"

"Oui?"

He spun around. She was standing almost even with him, as though having materialized from one of the trees. Feeling like a complete fool now, he clumsily untied his bow tie. "What are you, a nymph or something?"

She laughed, a breathy, stirring sound. "I'm quite human, flesh and blood, just like you."

He loosed the collar button of his pleated shirt, but then his fingers fell still. Again he was arrested by her remarkable uniqueness. His eyes started at the top of her sleek head and moved over her face, along her graceful neck, across her full breasts, and down the center of her enticing body.

"Human, yes. Flesh and blood, definitely." He took enough steps to bring him toe to toe with her. "But just like me? No. Hell no. You're like nobody I've ever seen before."

He had to touch her again to reassure himself that she was real. He touched the curve of her breast first, that smooth expanse swelling above the neckline of her dress almost even with the notch of her shoulder. It was as marvelous to touch as it was to look at. He rubbed it lightly with the knuckle of his index finger.

Then he slid his fingertip up and down her neck and followed it up to her exquisitely chiseled jawbone. When his hand curved around the nape of her neck, she relaxed it and let her head bend back slightly, offering her lips up to the first soft brushing caress of his.

The fruity alcohol was sweet on her breath. Its essence filled his head, aroused his body, inflamed his passions. His tongue flicked along her lips. He groaned her name, a name as enchanting as she.

In response, she placed her hand inside his jacket and laid it on the muscled wall of his chest. His lips parted above hers, pressed, then kissed her in earnest as his other arm closed around her waist.

She was as pliant as damp sand, conforming her body to fit the shape of his. Scout felt the firm thrust of her breasts, the delectable softness of her femininity, the suppleness of her thighs. His skull exploded with desire. He moved one hand to her breast and caressed it through her dress. Beneath the soft cloth he felt her nipple harden against the circular motions of his thumb.

His tongue entered her mouth hungrily. Time and again he sampled her taste, withdrawing his tongue to savor the delicacy of her lips, dipping again into the dark, sweet recess of her mouth.

His heart hammered painfully in his chest. His sex, heavy and thick, throbbed with each heartbeat. He nestled it in her cleft. His hand cupped her derriere and tilted her up and forward against him, wondering what she would think of his full hardness and hoping that she would respond favorably.

He moaned with gratification when he felt her hand fumbling between their bodies at waist level, obviously in search of his zipper tab.

That's why he was stunned to feel something hard and cold being shoved into his midriff. No sooner had that startling realization registered than she pulled free of him and stepped out of reach.

"What the hell is—"

The question froze on his lips when he lowered his gaze to the pistol, the barrel of which was aimed straight at his belly button.

Scout gaped at her. "What the hell are you doing?"

"I'm pointing a pistol at you, Mr. Ritland," she stated calmly in her accented English. "And unless you do everything I say, I'm prepared to shoot you."

Her expression was deadly serious, but Scout found it difficult to take her threat at face value. There were plenty of adjectives to describe her, but menacing wasn't among them.

"Shoot me? For what?" he asked, guffawing. "For kissing you?"

"For wrongly presuming that I wanted to be kissed and pawed like a waterfront prostitute."

He propped his hands on his hips. "What was I supposed to think after you lured me out here?"

"I didn't *lure* you."

"The hell you didn't," he said, his temper flaring.

"You followed me. I didn't encourage you."

His amusement had vanished. "Don't pull that self-righteous crap on me, princess. You wanted me to follow you. Your rejection was your come-on. You liked the kiss and everything else," he said with a sly glance down at her breasts and their projecting centers. "You can't very well pretend you didn't when I can plainly see otherwise."

Her eyes went dangerously bright and she pulled herself up to military erectness. "This isn't about your kisses."

"Then what?"

"You'll find out soon enough. Turn around and start walking."

He snorted another laugh as he peered into the

impenetrable foliage surrounding them. "Forgive the cliché, but it's a jungle out there."

"Walk, Mr. Ritland."

"Like hell."

"Need I remind you that I've got you at gunpoint and you'd be wise to do as I say?"

His lips curled into an arrogant smirk. "Oh, I'm real scared," he whispered tauntingly. "A woman who looks like a goddess and kisses like an expensive whore is dangerous, all right. But her weapon of choice is not a handgun."

Outraged, she cried, "How dare you—"

He lunged for the pistol. They wrestled for control of it.

Chantal gave a small, surprised exclamation as the gun went off in her hand. They stood frozen, staring at each other with incredulity. Then Scout staggered back a step and looked down at his thigh. It was pumping blood.

"You shot me," he said, stupidly stating the obvious. Then, angrily, "You shot me! You actually shot me!"

The delayed pain finally slammed into him. It had the impetus of a major leaguer's pitch finding the center of the catcher's mitt. Lights exploded around him. He gaped at his wound, gaped at the woman, then issued the roar of an enraged beast and lunged for her again.

This time the pain came crashing down on the base of his skull. He collapsed onto the spongy jungle floor. Overhead, through the trees, he saw colored lights flashing and popping like an electric kaleidoscope.

Then the night edged in and blotted out everything.

Two

Chantal was horrified by this unexpected turn of events. *"Mon Dieu!* Why did you strike him, André?"

The man who had crept up behind Scout knelt down beside him now. "I was afraid he would hurt you."

"I was handling it. How badly is he injured?"

"I struck him hard enough only to knock him unconscious."

When Chantal saw the self-doubt registered in the man's eyes, she modified her critical tone. "I know you reacted out of concern for me. Thank you. But now we must deal with this."

She, too, was kneeling and bending over the unconscious engineer. She rifled through his most accessible pockets until one yielded a handkerchief and used it to form a tourniquet around his thigh above the bullet wound. His blood stained the front of her dress. "He's bleeding heavily."

"The jeep isn't far. I'll carry him."

The young islander was agile and wiry, though he wasn't very tall, not anywhere close to Ritland's height. With an effort he hefted the man over one shoulder and, with Chantal's help, struggled to his feet.

"He doesn't look as heavy as he is."

"He's very muscular."

Her remark caused André to glance at her curiously. She hastily looked away. She knew Scout was muscular because she had caressed the taut muscles beneath his tuxedo shirt, felt the power in his thighs, and sensed the strength under his leanness.

Before they started through the jungle, she examined the back of Scout's head where a goose egg was forming. As her fingers moved through his thick brown hair, he moaned.

"We must hurry, André," she said, slipping out of her high-heel sandals.

"Oui."

They moved soundlessly through the jungle, though no one from the resort could have heard them over the orchestra's exuberant rendition of "Yankee Doodle Dandy." Fireworks were still exploding over the lagoon, the same pyrotechnics that had kept the gunshot from being heard.

"I'll sit in the back with him." Upon reaching the jeep, Chantal scrambled into the backseat. André placed Scout's slumped form beside her. She laid his head in her lap; his legs were folded into the small area between the seats. André got behind the wheel and started the engine. Within seconds they were under way.

Scout remained blessedly unconscious, although every time the jeep found a pothole, which was frequently, he groaned with pain. Chantal stared down into his face, not liking how pale it had become. His beard stubble looked unusually dark against his pallor.

The kidnapping had been planned. The shooting had not. Machismo, first Scout's then André's, had resulted in needless violence which she found repulsive and frightening.

She had shot a man! What if he lost so much blood that he died? What if she couldn't extract the bullet without damaging a nerve and leaving him permanently lame? What if she couldn't extract it at all?

The what-ifs got more horrendous with each mile. André was driving with painstaking care for their injured passenger, but also with necessary speed.

Covering the distance to the remote side of the island in broad daylight was a challenge. In darkness the highways were nightmarish hazards that dwindled to dirt roads winding through forested mountains with sheer cliffs falling away into the ocean below.

Once, André had to jarringly apply the brakes to avoid hitting a goat crossing the road. Scout groaned and mumbled an obscenity. Protectively, apologetically, Chantal clasped his head tightly to her breasts.

His trousers were saturated with blood. Without even stopping to think about it, she wiggled out of her dress, wadded it up, and pressed it against the oozing bullet hole.

She thought nothing of being bare-breasted until Scout rolled his head toward her. His face nuzzled her breasts. She felt the rasp of his beard against her skin, his lips against her nipples. Alarmed by the sensations that speared through her, she whipped the hibiscus blossoms from her hair and shook it free. The straight black, heavy strands rippled down over her breasts to her waist, covering her as adequately as a thin shirt would.

When at last they reached the bridge, André brought the jeep to a stop. Together, Chantal and he lifted Scout out. André supported his head and shoulders while she took his feet. They started across the swaying suspension footbridge.

The villagers, instinctively alerted to trouble, began pouring from their huts, though it was the middle of the night. Torches appeared on the other side of the bridge. Chantal called out for help. The moment they reached the other side of the deep gorge, the trio was surrounded by curious, chattering villagers.

She called for one of the men to take Scout's feet. "Bring him quickly," she urged in rapid French, then ran ahead up the incline to the house that was set apart from the rest of the village. She crossed the wide veranda, shoved open the door, and reached for the nearest lantern.

By the time she had it lit, Ritland was being carried through the front door. "In the back. Quickly, quickly."

The injured man was placed on a long table in a spare, unfurnished room in the rear portion of the house that was often used for medical emergencies. Chantal turned her patient's head to one side and examined the knot on the back of his skull. It was solid but hadn't enlarged.

"He'll be fine if I can remove that bullet without any complications." She was thinking out loud as she anxiously pulled her lower lip through her teeth. "And if he doesn't lose too much blood in the meantime. If the femoral artery . . . Cut off his clothing while I scrub."

She scrubbed her hands and forearms with an antiseptic solution, as she had seen her father do, then donned a clean white smock over her panties, which was all she had arrived in. None of the villagers had taken notice.

When she turned, the man she had kidnapped was lying naked on the table. The gaping, bloody hole in his left thigh was a hideous sight. The wound needed immediate attention. Her father wasn't here, so, though surgery wasn't her field, the grisly task fell to her. She was relieved to see that a native woman who often helped her father with these procedures had arrived and was mopping Scout with disinfectant from knees to ribs.

Chantal filled a syringe with morphine and injected it into her patient's vein. "I can't spare any more for now," she told her somber audience. "André, please stay. I may need you to hold him down. Nikki, you're in charge of the lanterns. See that I've got plenty of light at all times."

"Oui, mademoiselle."

She arranged a tray of sterilized utensils, set it within reach, and tied a mask over the lower part of her face, directing the others around the table who were assisting to do likewise. Next she draped Scout's leg with clean towels, leaving an open area in which to work.

If only her father were here, she thought as she picked up a scalpel.

But he wasn't, and a man's life hung in the balance. It would be her fault, in more ways than one, if he died. This was by far the most ambitious surgical procedure she'd ever attempted, and she was terrified of making a blunder that would permanently damage him. But his death was certain if she didn't try.

Before she probed the wound, she prayed to the Christian God. Then, for good measure, she prayed to the gods who were believed to protect the village and its people.

Now wasn't the time to chance offending any deity.

Scout was laid on a narrow bed in an extra bedroom in the house. For days Chantal hardly left the room. She remained at the bedside, monitoring his moans and groans, blotting sweat from his body, checking beneath the bandage for signs of infection.

Though many offered to sit with him while she rested, she refused. The man lying beneath the single sheet consumed her time and all her thoughts. Her prayers revolved around him.

She gave him penicillin injections to ward off infection. It distressed her that she couldn't give him more than one injection of morphine for his pain. When that dose began to wear off, when Scout began to toss his head and mumble incoherently, when his eyelids began to flicker and he began to flail his arms, she plied him with the locally fermented alcohol.

She would lift his head off the pillow and hold it against her breasts while she tipped a cup toward his lips, which she kept moist with cocoa butter. The liquor would be dribbled slowly into his mouth until he had drunk it all. She bathed his perspiring face and body with cool water.

During all this she tried not to dwell on his attractiveness, but on the severity of his condition. Smoothing the cocoa butter on his lips naturally made her recall his kiss, how expert and delicious it had been . . . and how much he would hate her for the way she had tricked him.

It was then that she entertained doubts about her actions. What she had done was daring, risky, and undeniably illegal, but she'd been left with no choice. One got desperate when one's options ran out.

Sitting beside his sickbed, staring into his bearded face, she fervently hoped that once she explained the situation, Scout would come to understand her desperation and feel charitable toward her.

In the evening of the third day she realized that he hadn't moved his injured leg. She began to fear that she had damaged a nerve when she extracted the

bullet, which had been firmly imbedded in the mus-
cle. To check, she jabbed a straight pin into his big
toe. He not only flinched, he jerked his knee up to
his chest and screamed an expletive before relaxing
his leg again.

Chantal decided it was time to let him wake up.

He stared at the ceiling for several moments. From
where she sat in the straight-back chair near the
bed, she could tell that he was trying to orient himself.

Eventually, with a deep sigh he turned his head
on the pillow and spotted her through the veil of
mosquito netting. He blinked. "You?" he croaked.

"Chantal duPont," she said, barely above a whisper.

Even so, he winced. "You don't have to shout." He
wet his lips with his tongue and obviously tasted
the salve she had been lubricating them with. Experimentally, he touched his tongue to them again.
"Where am I?"

"Don't you remember what happened?"

With an effort he shook his head, focused on her
again, and tried to sit up. Groaning, he flopped
back on the pillow. "Jeez," he said raspily, raising
his hand to cover his eyes, "my head's coming off.
We must've had a helluva party last night."

He didn't remember. But given time, he would.
She waited. Suddenly she saw his body grow taut.
Gradually, he lowered his hand from his bloodshot
eyes. They found her again. This time they were
glaring balefully. Three days growth of beard made
him look dangerous.

"I'm not lying here buck naked and hung over
because we had an all-night orgy, am I?"

She shook her head, sending a curtain of ebony
hair shimmering over her back.

He hissed a curse, then released a thin breath of

air as he localized the source of his pain. She watched his hand search for his wound beneath the sheet. When he encountered the gauze bandage wrapped around his thigh, he fixed her with another murderous stare.

"Now I remember. You shot me."

"It was an accident," she said hastily.

"The hell it was."

"I held you at gunpoint, but I wanted only to threaten you. I didn't even know the gun was loaded."

"It was your gun. You took it out of your purse."

"I told André to find me a gun. He didn't tell me he'd put bullets in it."

Scout raised his hand to his forehead again. "Who the hell is—"

"André. He's the man who clouted you on the head."

"Well, he did a damn good job." Scout groaned.

"I didn't know he was going to do that, either."

"I think my cranium is fractured."

"No, it's not. Part of that is the liquor."

"Liquor?"

"I've been giving it to you to keep you unconscious."

"Why?"

"Because I knew you'd be in pain. We're low on morphine, and it's hard to get because I'm—"

He raised his hand wearily to stave off further explanations which he couldn't yet grasp. His eyes closed. Chantal left her chair, moved aside the netting, and bent over him. She tested his forehead for fever. There was none. His skin was cool if a bit clammy. His eyes came open again.

"How serious was the wound?"

"Not too bad. I removed the bullet."

"*You* removed the bullet?"

"Thankfully, it didn't sever the artery or damage the bone or nerves." She didn't tell him how she knew that. Somehow she sensed he wouldn't appreciate knowing she had pricked his big toe with a pin. "Your leg will be stiff for a while, but in a few weeks it will be fine." Picking up a china teapot from the tray on the nightstand, she poured some of the steeping brew into a cup. "Drink this."

He sniffed suspiciously. "What is it? Drugs? Liquor?"

"Broth with herbs and healing elements. You need it to regain your strength. You lost a lot of blood, and I had no way to give you a transfusion." She pressed the cup against his lips, but he refused to drink.

"Why didn't you take me to the hospital?"

"I couldn't do that," she exclaimed, incredulous. "I would have had to explain the gunshot, and they would have arrested me."

"Yeah, well, that's the risk you take when you kidnap and shoot somebody, princess."

"I'm willing to accept the consequences of what I did. Only later, when I no longer need you. Now please drink this. For the nourishment."

Querulously, he shoved the cup away. "Why'd you shanghai me?"

"I told you. I need you."

"Why, what's wrong with you?"

She shook her head with perplexity. "I don't understand."

"That you have to shoot a guy to get him naked and in bed with you."

Her blue eyes turned dark with disapproval. She was tempted to unman him by dumping the scalding contents of the cup into his lap. Only her concern for his overall physical condition kept her from doing so.

"Drink this or I'll have to force it down you," she said with the same imperious tone with which she had said, "Walk, Mr. Ritland," a few days earlier.

Holding her stare, he sipped. Then he spat, cursing liberally. "What the hell is that stuff?"

"We couldn't butcher one of our few cows just for you. It's full of protein. Drink it."

"I thought you said it was broth. If it's not beef broth, what is it?"

"It's good for you."

"What is it, I said."

"Drink it," she stubbornly repeated.

"All right," he consented after a silent contest of wills, "I will. But only because I want to recover enough strength to get out of this bed and strangle you." Unperturbed by his threat, she held the cup to his lips. He drank the entire contents, shuddering with distaste.

"More?"

"That's all I can stomach for now." Before she could move away, he grabbed a handful of her shirt and pulled her down to within inches of his angry face.

"I can tell I'm about to pass out again. Before I do, tell me why you did this to me. Why, for chrissake?"

She gazed directly into his eyes. "You're going to build me a bridge, Mr. Ritland."

She watched the disbelief spread across his features seconds before his eyelids fluttered, then sank shut. His fingers, still gripping the gauzy fabric of her blouse, relaxed and eventually let go. His head collapsed back onto the pillow.

Well, now he knew.

Three

The room was bathed in lavender light when he woke up again. There was no glass in the windows, only louvered shutters. They had been opened. There was a breeze. He could smell the ocean. He could hear it.

The bullet wound no longer felt like a branding iron gouging his thigh, but it was aching dully and persistently. He was very thirsty. The broth he'd drunk had left the inside of his mouth feeling furry . . . or perhaps the unpleasant texture was a souvenir of the liquor he'd drunk, willingly or unwillingly.

He was muzzy, but there was no longer thunder inside his head as there had been earlier today. Yesterday? Dammit, he didn't know what day it was or how long it had been since the gala opening of the Coral Reef resort. Where the hell was he, anyway?

He turned his head, then started with surprise.

Three women were standing at the foot of his bed just outside the mosquito netting. One was young, slender, and quite pretty. One was pleasantly plump and not quite as attractive. One had a face that would stop a clock. They were wearing short, colorful sarongs around their hips but nothing on top. It was a most disconcerting sight.

When they realized he was awake and looking at them, they began to giggle and speak among themselves in hushed, excited French. Self-consciously he reached for the sheet and pulled it higher to cover his bare torso.

"Where's what's-her-name? The princess? Chantal?" he asked hoarsely.

That simple and seemingly innocent question brought on a chorus of giggles. Scout realized that he was the topic of their conversation. They kept casting covert glances at him, followed by bursts of laughter that were doing his headache no good at all.

"Could I have something to drink, please?"

"You may."

He angled his head toward the door in time to see his kidnapper enter, bearing a tray with a tall pitcher of water and a drinking glass on it. "I predicted you'd be thirsty." To the women, she said, "*Merci*," and continued speaking to them in soft French.

"What's going on?"

"They insisted that I needed a rest," she told him as she pulled aside the netting, "so they volunteered to watch you while I bathed and napped. I was thanking them for taking such good care of you."

He supposed her recent bath accounted for the smell of flowers that accompanied her into the room. The longest, silkiest, darkest head of hair he'd ever craved to run his fingers through was still damp.

One of the island women began speaking with animation. The other two covered their mouths, trying unsuccessfully to stifle their giggles.

"Now what?" Scout asked Chantal, who was moving around his bed, straightening the sheet, and tucking it beneath the mattress. She avoided looking at him. "They, uh, said you were perspiring, so they sponged you off for me."

He addressed the women. *"Merci."* They collapsed upon each other, made weak with laughter. "What's so damn funny? What's the matter, didn't I pronounce it right?"

"Oui," Chantal replied, again avoiding his gaze. The corners of her lips were twitching with the need to smile.

The whispered jabbering grated on Scout's nerves, especially since he knew it was about him. "What are they talking about now?"

"You."

"I *know* that much. What are they saying?" He caught Chantal's hand. "Is there something wrong with my leg? You didn't cut it off while I was unconscious, did you?" He lifted the sheet and checked to see that the limb was intact.

With annoyance she pulled her hand free of his and poked a thermometer beneath his tongue. "If you must know, they're fascinated by your hair."

"My hair?" he mumbled around the thermometer while raising an inquisitive hand to his head.

"Your body hair."

Scout almost swallowed the thermometer before he jerked it from between his lips and reflexively reached for the sheet again. "My *what*?"

"The island men don't have chest hair. Yours is"— she faltered and swallowed hard—"quite plentiful, Mr. Ritland."

For a doctor, she sure did seem shy to Scout. On the other hand, he reflected, if she was accustomed to treating only island men, it stood to reason she could be skittish about his hairy chest.

"Are they necessary?" he asked, nodding toward his bare-breasted audience. "Isn't it enough that I'm subjected to you?"

Chantal thanked the trio of gigglers and ushered them toward the door. As their bare feet whispered across the smooth hardwood floor, they continued to chatter like colorful birds.

"Jeez, this is maddening. What are they saying now?"

"You don't speak French?"

"I can order from a menu if it's standard fare. This ninety-mile-an-hour stuff escapes me."

On the brink of laughter herself, she raised her index finger to her lips and shushed the women. Then to Scout she said, "They're saying that I'm very lucky to be tending you."

"Why?"

"Because . . . because you are the village's honored guest."

"Bull." He knew enough about human nature to recognize when he was being lied to. The blue-eyed doll face was devious. He'd learned that the hard way. He wasn't getting the full truth.

Suddenly his ears picked up a familiar word. Springing upright, he pointed at the woman currently speaking and exclaimed, "I caught that! I know that word. That's . . . that's . . ." He snapped his fingers rapidly as his memory slogged through the bog of the last few days of unconsciousness. "That's that statue. The guy with the wicked grin and huge—"

His eyes sprang up to Chantal's. She hastily turned her back to him and shooed the women from the room. Following them out, she remained gone for several moments. When she returned, she moved to the nightstand and poured a glass of water from the pitcher. She appeared cool and unruffled, but there was a telltale pink stain in her cheeks.

"Would you care for water, Mr. Ritland?"

He took the glass from her and drank, eyeing her with no small degree of admiration. This woman was in control at all times.

Or was she? He had to test it, had to find out.
Knowing an enemy's strengths and weaknesses was
the first step toward defeating him.

As he passed the glass back to her, he touched her
fingertips and asked silkily, "Who gave me my sponge
baths before the three stooges took over?"

"I did, Mr. Ritland." Her gaze was unwavering.

"Oh, yeah?"

"More water?"

"No thanks. Not for now, but leave the pitcher."

She returned the glass to the tray and, since the
sun had completely set by now, lit the lantern. "You
can spare each of us the embarrassment of an attempted seduction, Mr. Ritland. It won't work. I
took desperate measures to get you here. I can't be
romanced into letting you go until you're finished."

Her cool, calm, and collected manner annoyed him
as much as what she said. He threw back the sheet
and swung his legs over the side of the bed. The
pain that coursed through his thigh, and from there
to every nerve ending in his body, made him nause-
ated. Gritting his teeth, he swayed with dizziness.
He was as weak as a kitten and had to brace his
arms on the edge of the thin mattress to remain
upright.

"I'll get out of here," he said through his teeth,
which were clenched in agony and rage.

"You'll find your chances negligible, especially since
you won't be able even to walk for several days." He
could almost sense compassion in her melodic voice.
"You don't remember the drive here, but the Coral
Reef resort is on the other side of the island. Between here and there the terrain is mountainous,
undeveloped, and unpopulated. The roads are little
more than goat trails. The village has only one jeep.
It belongs to my father and has been carefully hidden from you. None of the villagers could be bribed

into showing you where it is. Please don't offend them by trying. On foot, *one* foot, you wouldn't stand a chance of making it back to what you would call civilization."

"Watch me, princess."

She merely smiled. "Have it your way. Are you hungry?"

"I could eat a horse."

"Good. That's what you're having."

She left him gaping at the empty doorway. Beneath his breath he cursed his pain, his weakness, the culpability that had gotten him in this fix in the first place.

He should have known from the start that she was just too good to be true. What an idiot he'd been! If he hadn't been so randy, so tipsy on that lethal local liquor, he would have proceeded with more caution. But no, like a damn fool he'd jumped in with both feet and now he was in way over his head.

Though it took a tremendous amount of effort and strength that he didn't have, he remained sitting on the edge of the bed. Somehow that made him feel less helpless. Lying down, he was really at her mercy.

She returned carrying another tray. It had the teapot he recognized and a glass of milky substance.

"I'm not drinking any more of that swill," he said stubbornly, hoping his voice carried more impetus than he felt.

"Then I'll have to force-feed you."

He watched grimly as she poured some of the steaming brew into a cup. "Is it really broth made from horse meat?"

"That's considered a delicacy in many parts of the world."

"So's dog meat. I don't plan to eat any of that, either."

"This horse gave up his life for you. The least you could do is show your appreciation."

"If you wouldn't slaughter a cow for me, why a horse?"

"Actually," she said, frowning slightly, "the poor creature was found in a roadside ditch already dead. But he was discovered before the meat had begun to spoil."

"Forget it, Florence Nightingale." He pushed aside the extended cup.

She flashed him an enchanting smile. "You want to build up enough strength to strangle me, don't you? Or have you changed your mind?"

He yanked the cup from her and in the process sloshed some of the scalding liquid onto his chest. "Ouch, jeez!"

Chantal responded quickly by reaching for a linen napkin on the tray and using it to blot up the drops sprinkling his chest hair. As she leaned forward, strands of her hair slid over her shoulder and brushed across his lap, which he had meagerly covered with a corner of the sheet.

His gut tightened with sexual awareness. The feel of her hair on his belly and thighs was like being caressed with black satin ribbons. She might be crazy as a bedbug, even dangerous, but he still wanted to stroke her hair, her skin, and kiss her all over.

He made a fist around the skein of hair and lifted it off his lap. Her hand poised inches above his chest; her eyes connected with his. Their faces were close. He could feel her rapid breath against his face, soughing between moist, parted lips. Damn, he wanted that mouth beneath his again.

"My chest is fine," he said tightly.

She straightened and dropped the napkin back onto the tray. He quickly dispensed with the vile broth, making a horrible face as he swallowed the last of it. "When can I have something solid? Or is part of your plan to keep me weak from hunger, giving me only horse broth to keep me alive?"

"No. I want you strong as soon as possible."

"So I can . . . what was it? Build you a bridge?"

"That's right," she replied, all seriousness.

"You've been out in the tropical sun too long, princess," he said, laughing. "I'm not building anything except an airtight criminal case against you. Since the end of World War Two, Parrish Island has been a United States territory, you know. Pagan and primitive as it is," he said, glancing at the kerosene lantern, "all the laws of the land still apply. You're going to jail just as soon as I can put you there."

"Perhaps. But first you'll build my bridge."

"What bridge? And what the hell's that?" he demanded cantankerously as she tried to foist on him the other glass she had carried in.

"Coconut milk. You'll like it."

He drank that. After the broth, it tasted as good and satisfying as a milk shake. "Okay, I drank it. Now answer my question."

"What question?"

"What bridge do you keep referring to?"

"We'll talk about that in the morning. Do you have to go to the bathroom?"

"So bad I'm almost teary-eyed."

"You should have said so." She reached beneath the bed and came up with a porcelain basin.

Scout looked at it, looked at her, and felt his cheeks growing warm. "Like hell."

"It's a little foolish to get modest now, Mr. Ritland, since I've been taking care of you for days. You have no secrets from me. Use the basin or suffer the consequences."

He gnawed on the inside of his cheek. She appeared determined. His body certainly was. "Would a little privacy be asking too much?"

She turned on her heel and left the room. Great legs, he thought, following her retreat with his eyes. She was wearing ordinary shorts, not the sarongs the native women had had on. And Scout was almost relieved that she had on a top. Her camp shirt was made of sheer cotton. She had knotted the tails of it at her waist. From the soft swaying motion of her breasts each time she moved, he would bet his last nickel that she wasn't wearing anything underneath it.

But the shirt was there, and he was glad. It would be hard to remain furious at her if she were going around topless. He was having a hard enough time remaining unemotional about her bare legs and feet.

She knocked before coming in again. Humiliated beyond anything he'd ever experienced, he pouted while she efficiently dispensed with the contents of the bedpan.

"I think you should lie down, Mr. Ritland. You're getting pale." She placed a hand on each of his shoulders and attempted to ease him back.

One arm whipped out and encircled her waist. The other shot up and he captured a handful of her hair near her scalp. He saw her wince, but relaxed his grip only slightly.

"Did you pick me at random?" he asked through lips turning white with pain, anger, and frustration.

"No."

"Those come-hither glances you were transmitting loud and clear didn't have anything to do with you liking my looks, did they? You didn't pick me from the crowd because you thought I was attractive."

"This will be a blow to your ego, Mr. Ritland, but no, it wouldn't have mattered what you looked like."

"You set me up from the beginning."

"Yes."

"You had me picked out beforehand and you made damn sure I noticed you at that party."

"That's right."

His arm tightened around her waist and hauled her closer. Her legs bumped his, but all he noticed was how cool and smooth her skin felt. He hardly felt the stab of pain.

"Why, dammit? Tell me."

"I've told you. For the bridge."

"What freaking bridge?"

She wriggled away from him and tossed her hair over her shoulder all in one aggravated motion. "I'll explain it when you're stronger, possibly in the morning."

Keeping his eyes on hers, he allowed her to push him back on the bed. Once he was settled, she made certain fresh water was within his reach and that the netting was covering the bed, then extinguished the lantern.

He could hear her bare feet on the polished plank floor as he watched her silhouette slip from the room.

Scout stared into the darkness for a long time, but he didn't fall asleep. He didn't even relax. His mind was in such turmoil, he couldn't.

He berated himself for being such a sap. Why the hell was he allowing this situation to continue? She was crafty, true, but he was no moron. Actually, a good many people considered him rather astute.

He outsized her by seventy or eighty pounds. She was noticeably taller than the island women, but he remembered that even wearing high heels, she had come only to his chin. They were of complementary heights, a perfect fit for kissing, for . . .

"Hell." He cursed into the darkness, which was relieved only by the moonlight pouring in through the window. He didn't want to think about the kiss, or he would substantiate the women's comparison of him to the horny little idol. Besides, it was his predicament that demanded his attention.

Chantal duPont seemed to wield a lot of power and prestige around there, but he didn't see armed guards posted outside his door. How difficult could it be to overpower her and demand that she take her father's jeep out of hiding and drive him back to the civilized side of the island?

And where was the pistol she'd shot him with? He sure as hell wasn't going to locate it by lying in this bed, a bed better suited to a Lilliputian.

With that thought he rebelliously tossed back the sheet and netting and sat up. This time he eased his legs over the side of the bed. It caused his left one to throb hotly.

When he stood up, dangling his injured leg inches above the floor, he realized again that he was naked. He reached for a towel on the nightstand and wrapped it around his waist. Not much, but better than nothing.

Earlier he had spotted a broom propped in one corner of the room. It was in that direction that he hopped on his right foot, using pieces of furniture as supports along the way.

By the time he reached the corner, sweat had popped out on his brow and he was breathing through his mouth as though he'd run ten miles uphill. Using the broom as a makeshift crutch, he headed for the door. Due to his dizziness, it appeared to be listing several degrees off-center.

The house was silent. The only sound was the incessant swishing of the ocean. It wasn't far away. He searched first for any signs of electricity but, as he expected, there were none. Nor was there a telephone.

The house, however, was well furnished, spotlessly clean, and filled with personal objects. There seemed to be books everywhere, stacked on tables, on shelves, even on the floor. Some were in French, some English.

As soundlessly as possible he made painful, halting progress through the large living room and down a hallway, past a bedroom where the bed was turned down but unoccupied, to another large room that was divided by a carved screen to form a combination bedroom and study.

The large bed was unoccupied, but Chantal was sitting alone in the study area. A kerosene lamp, burning low, cast deep shadows across her face. She was half reclining in a leather chair with her bare feet propped on the corner of a messy, paper-strewn desk. She was wearing eyeglasses. An open book was lying in her lap. Her concentration on it was so intent that she didn't see or hear him approach.

Her hair was hanging like a thick curtain over the back of the chair, but a few strands framed her flawless cheeks. She had unbuttoned and untied her blouse, as though she'd started to take it off before changing her mind.

Seeing the perfect slope of her breasts, tipped with nipples that were designed for a man's mouth to enjoy, made something besides Scout's bullet wound throb with pressure and heat.

He tried to push prurient thoughts aside, but his voice was thick and husky when he picked up their previous conversation where they had left off.

"You'll explain it to me now."

She jumped. Her feet hit the floor. The book slid from her lap. Her head snapped up. Through the large lenses of her glasses she distinguished his form in the deep shadows of the room. It took several seconds and his hot stare for her to realize that her blouse was gaping open. She snatched the sides of it together to cover herself and whipped off her glasses.

"Mr. Ritland, how did you manage—"

"Drop the Mr. Ritland routine, okay? I'm not a formal guest in your home. I'm your prisoner. You've seen me naked and I've wished you were, especially when my tongue was sliding in and out of your mouth and I was massaging your nipple. I think that puts us on a first-name basis, don't you?"

He took perverse enjoyment in seeing how much his sardonic speech had offended her. At the same time, he marveled over his crudeness. At home he wouldn't have dreamed of talking like that to a woman, any woman. He had read of men who reverted to savagery when they were separated from civilization and society as they knew it, but he hadn't expected it of himself. Ever. But especially not so soon.

Then again, he'd been severely provoked by this woman with the breathtaking blue eyes, now eloquently searching his face as though looking for and expecting an apology. Frustrated, he released a gust of air. Her wounded expression made *him* feel like the bad guy.

"At least grant that I've got a good reason to be angry and upset."

"You do," she conceded quietly. "I honestly didn't mean to shoot you. I'm sorry."

"Well, it's done now, isn't it? What's this about a bridge?"

"Are you sure you're up to hearing the explanation tonight?"

"I'm sure."

"Then please sit down." Smiling, she added, "Scout."

Gratefully, he collapsed into a chair facing hers.

Four

Even in the faint lantern light Chantal could see how chalky his lips were. She knew he was in pain. In his weakened condition, covering the distance from the bedroom he occupied had been tantamount to a journey. His skin looked gray and clammy, and his forehead was beaded with sweat. It had dampened the dark brown strands of hair that fell over his brows.

But clearer than fatigue and agony, he emanated determination. She reasoned that she had kept him uninformed long enough. Where to begin?

"You don't remember because you were unconscious," she told him, "but when you arrived here, André and I carried you across a footbridge that spans a deep gorge. This gorge separates the village from the island proper. The bridge is a hazard. It desperately needs to be replaced. I brought you here to build my people a new bridge."

She watched him as he mentally digested her remarks. His expression remained impassive, but she saw a telltale spark of interest in his eyes. Nice eyes. Light golden-brown eyes.

She averted her attention from them and caught him mindlessly massaging the area just above the bandage on his thigh.

"Are you in pain?"

He ceased rubbing his thigh and made a querulous face. "No," he lied.

"I could give you something."

"No way, Miss duPont. Whenever you give me something, I tend to remain unconscious for the next several hours."

"An aspirin?"

"Tell me about the bridge," he said impatiently. "I don't suppose we're talking about a short little bridge here."

She made a dismissive gesture and tried to sound casual. "A couple hundred feet or so."

"Jeez." He started to laugh and shook his head.

Annoyed, Chantal snapped, "I'm glad you find this all so amusing. I can assure you that to my people this bridge means life. My people—"

"*Your* people?" he shouted. "Just who the hell are you, anyway?"

Considering that a fair question, she replied, "Chantal duPont."

"That much I know." He was rubbing his leg again, but seemed unaware of it. When he caught her watching him, he stopped. "Are you a high priestess around here? Royalty? A missionary? What?"

His guesses brought a smile to her lips. "Nothing that grandiose. I was born here in the village." Reaching for a silver picture frame, she turned it toward him. "My father, my mother."

He picked up the frame and looked at the pictures curiously. Chantal closely gauged his reaction to the Caucasian man and the Polynesian woman. When he set the frame back on the desk, he remarked, "You have your father's eyes. But the rest of you is your mother."

"Thank you. She was very beautiful."

"Was?"

"She died years ago." She stared at the photograph of the lovely, gentle face captured in the picture. "I know you're curious, though you're probably too polite to ask." He shifted uneasily in his chair, guiltily indicating that she was right.

"My father," Chantal began, "Dr. George duPont, served in the French Navy. He was stationed here on the island before the outbreak of the Second World War. The island, as you've probably noticed, is very seductive. After the war, France was in such a shambles, he returned here to work and study, although the island had by then become a U.S. territory. He met my mother, Lili, and fell in love with her. They were married."

"By the wistful look on your face, I gather they didn't live happily ever after," Scout said.

"Mother had been converted to Catholicism. Even so, when she accompanied my father back to France, she was shunned. Both of them were. The duPonts were an old and aristocratic family. It didn't seem to matter that they'd lost most of their fortune to the Nazis. The members of the family considered themselves part of the elite."

"Welcoming a Polynesian woman into the fold, embracing her as one of their own, was unthinkable."

Chantal lowered her head in acknowledgment. "Even though she carried a trace of French blood too." Whenever she dwelled on the prejudice her beautiful mother must have suffered, she ached for her. Chantal had experienced prejudice to a degree, and she was only half of what had alienated Lili from the duPonts and all her father's former friends and colleagues.

"So," she said, drawing in a ragged breath, "they returned to Parrish Island. My father continued his work and research here. He built this house, making it as modern as he was capable of doing with what was available. He introduced some modern amenities to the villagers. As a result, they came to depend on him to care for them."

"He became a father figure of sorts."

"Precisely."

"When did you come along? You're not that old."

"For years into their marriage my mother didn't conceive, which I've learned since then was a tremendous concern of hers. Finally she became pregnant with me. She wrote in her journal that the days she carried me inside her were the happiest of her life."

Her brows drew together. "But she was at an age where having a child is unsafe without expert prenatal care. The pregnancy was difficult. She never fully recovered from it. She died when I was very young. My memories of her are hazy, just a smiling face that often sang French lullabies to me."

They were quiet for several moments. Chantal was lost in her bittersweet reverie. Scout finally drew her out by asking, "Why didn't your father take you back to France after Lili's death?"

"By then this island was more his home than Paris. His work was here. He had adjusted to the unhurried pace of life. The villagers needed him. Besides," she added with a sad smile, "he wouldn't leave my mother."

"But he saw to it that you left."

"How did you know that?" she asked quickly, surprised.

He nodded behind her and she followed his gaze to the diplomas framed and mounted on the wall behind her. "A father's pride," she said with a Gallic shrug that came straight from George duPont. "I attended the English school on the military base."

"Which accounts for your command of the language."

"Thank you. When I graduated from high school, I was sent to California to college."

"Sent?"

"Kicking and screaming."

"Why? I'd think you'd want to see another part of the world."

Chantal tilted her head to one side, genuinely perplexed by the statement. "Why?" She spread her hands wide. "This is paradise. Everything I had learned in history classes taught me that in the rest of the world there were horrible wars and rebellions, suppression, slavery."

"You've got a point," Scout said grimly. "Why the United States and not France?"

"I had dual citizenship. For some reason Father thought America would be better for me than Europe."

"Was it?"

Chantal smiled and stood up. She moved to a liquor cabinet and poured a snifter of brandy. "Would you care for some?"

"No thanks. I'm swearing off."

"Once I got to the States, I discovered that it wasn't all bad. I discovered cheeseburgers, and rock music, and movies. To my surprise, I liked wearing fashionable clothes." She rolled the snifter back and forth between her palms while she subconsciously appreciated the woodsy bouquet of the brandy. "I wasn't totally innocent of such things, of course, because I'd spent time during high school on the military bases here."

"I'll bet the soldiers and sailors swarmed over you like drones around a queen bee."

Chantal sipped her brandy. Outwardly, she appeared calm, though Scout's teasing words churned up resentment. She had often been asked out, yes, but had learned soon enough to be wary of seemingly innocent dates.

Like all island girls, she had been considered easy prey to men far away from home and in need of female companionship. Several unpleasant experiences had been the origin of her distrust of Caucasian men, a distrust that had proven to be justified.

Because those memories were so upsetting, Chantal switched her attention back to Scout, who was staring at her with bemusement.

"What are you looking at?" she asked.

"Most men I know couldn't swizzle brandy that way. Did you learn how to drink from your father?"

She set aside the snifter, which she had been sipping at. "To drink and everything else."

"I can't figure it."

"What?"

"One minute you seem so sophisticated. The next—" He seemed to be arranging his thoughts. "After spending so much time in the States, why did you come back here?"

"I wanted to."

"You didn't like California?"

"Very much. There were many attractions to hold me in the States."

"So why'd you come back?"

"That's my business."

"Did your father urge you to return to Parrish Island?"

"He was certainly happy to see me back," she replied evasively, uneasy with discussing her personal life with Scout.

"Wasn't that rather selfish of him? He'd decided to spend his life here, but when you could have been practicing medicine in the States, it seems—"

"Medicine?" Their confused expressions were reflections of each other.

"Medicine," he repeated, nodding toward the degrees made out to Dr. Chantal Louise duPont. "Didn't you follow in your old man's footsteps and become a doctor?"

She began to laugh. "Yes, I followed in my old man's footsteps and became a doctor. We both have Ph.D.'s in geology."

Scout's face drained of what little color it had left. "Geology?" he croaked, squinting at the framed documents. Then, angrily swinging his eyes back to her, he repeated loudly, "*Geology!*"

He bounded from his chair. Chantal came out of hers a heartbeat later. "Be careful of—"

"You operated on my leg and you're not even a doctor?" he shouted.

"Would you rather have had me leave the bullet there? Let you bleed to death?"

He pointed down at the bandage on his thigh and yelled, "You operated on me. You could have cost me my leg. You could have left me a cripple for the rest of my life," he ranted. "Jeez! You're crazy!"

"Calm down. It wasn't that serious an operation. I have watched my father deal with injuries much worse than yours with successful results. I knew what to do even though I'd never done it."

"So he's a quack too."

"He dispenses antibiotics when he can get them and has done what was necessary to save someone's life, including surgery. He has set broken bones, removed tonsils and appendixes, assisted in difficult births. When the nearest hospital is on the other side of a mountain range, one learns to cope and to improvise."

"Not with *my* leg one doesn't improvise, princess!" He paused to draw several deep breaths, his chest rising and falling rapidly. "Where is your old man? I want to talk to him. I want to see him. Tonight," he said with crisp enunciation. "He's probably off his beam too. It sounds like insanity runs in the family.

But at this point my options are limited. I'll take my chances with him. Now, where is he?"

"He's not here."

He hopped toward her and gripped her by the shoulders, shaking her slightly. "Where is he?"

"He's somewhere in the foothills. Unavailable. But if he'd been here when I brought you in with a bullet in your thigh, he'd have done exactly as I did."

Scout hissed an expletive with such impetus, the vile word ghosted across Chantal's face. "I wouldn't have had a bullet in my thigh, I wouldn't have been brought here at all, if it weren't for you." He flung his hands off her.

"It isn't good for you to get upset like this." She realized, even if he didn't, that his curses had been spawned by pain as much as by fury. "Let me help you back to bed."

Leaving him no choice, she slipped her arm around his waist and hooked his arm around her neck. Shoving her shoulder up into his armpit, she took most of his weight upon herself.

"I can get back to bed on my own."

She glanced up at him. His white lips were pulled back, baring clenched teeth. His cheekbones appeared sharp and pronounced and were beaded with sweat. He was stubborn and proud to a fault.

"I'm sure you can," she said softly, "but it would take agonizing minutes and there's no need to put yourself through that when I'm here to help you."

His breath whistled through his teeth. "My leg hurts like hell."

"You shouldn't have gotten up."

"Well, I couldn't just lie there and let you run roughshod over me any longer."

Accidentally, he put weight down on his left foot. Groaning, he collapsed against her. She hugged him tighter, sliding her hand around him until it rested on the side of his ribs. His arm was still looped around her neck, his hand dangling in front of her chest. As he slumped forward, his fingertips grazed her breast, the very tip of it, which was already stiff and distended.

They froze. For several seconds each stared at the floor, unable to think, unable to breathe, unable to move. Chantal squeezed her eyes closed briefly, waiting for the sensations to stop rippling from her tightly beaded nipple into every other part of her body. Beneath her splayed hand the skin of his torso was warm. She could feel his heartbeat.

When she opened her eyes and would have begun walking, he remained still. Glancing up, she found him staring at something across the room. She followed his stare to the pistol, which she had placed on her father's nightstand.

"It wouldn't be worth the effort," she told him quietly, reading his thoughts. "I didn't know it was loaded when André procured it for me. I was so horrified over actually shooting you that I removed the bullets and threw them away."

With an air of defeat he sagged more heavily against her. Without further conversation they shuffled toward the room he'd left an hour earlier.

She eased him down to the side of the bed and turned to light the lantern. When she turned back around, he was ripping off the gauze bandage wrapped around his thigh.

"What are you doing?" she cried.

"What I should have done the second I regained consciousness from your alcoholic sabotage. For all I know, you've butchered me."

"Please don't."

When Chantal reached out to stay his hands, he batted them out of the way and ripped through the binding until it was lying in a tattered heap on the floor.

He seemed surprised by the neat row of stitches holding the incision together. The wound was clean, showing no signs of infection, though the area immediately encircling it was slightly swollen.

"I'm afraid you'll always have a scar," she said gently, "but it should make an interesting conversation piece."

He gave her a wry smile. "A scar I can live with. Gangrene would have been a little tough to take."

"Now that you've let air get to it, I'd better clean and bind it again. Would you rather be lying down?"

His eyes gradually moved up and locked with hers. Heat as penetrating and pleasurable as the tropical sun's rays rivered through her. Her knees went weak beneath the intensity of his stare.

Though she and her father had received an engraved invitation to the gala opening of the Coral Reef, attending had been a mission. She had gone purposefully to kidnap an engineer named Scout Ritland.

However, when André had surreptitiously pointed him out to her, her heart had skipped a beat and her stomach had tightened. His being handsome and sexy had certainly made an unpleasant task easier to execute.

Several times during that evening she had had to remind herself that her seduction of him wasn't genuine, that it was simply the means to an end that would determine the future of the village.

But frequently she had found herself rising to the challenge strictly as a woman in pursuit of the most attractive man at the party and regretting that it wouldn't culminate in a romantic interlude.

She knew from experience, however, that romance could result in terrible heartache. She had avoided it since the debacle in California. She would continue to do so even though the look Scout Ritland was giving her now had turned her dewy with desire and reminded her that she was a woman unfulfilled.

Assuming a professional air, she ignored his gaze and eased him back onto the pillows. He continued to stare at her unwaveringly, but she avoided looking into his face and concentrated on swabbing the incision with antiseptic. Then, bending his knee up, she wrapped it with fresh gauze.

"You really should take an analgesic."

"Forget it. Dealing with you requires a clear head and all my faculties."

"A brandy?"

His eyebrow arched suspiciously. "Straight brandy? No Mickey Finn?"

She frowned down at him, then left the room, returning in under a minute with a snifter of brandy. Scout took it from her and sipped. He closed his eyes as he swallowed and let out a pleasurable sigh.

"Your old man has expensive taste," he remarked, making a satisfied smack.

He absently rubbed his bare stomach, where, she knew from experience, the brandy was spreading a delicious, languid warmth. His fingers moved through the soft, silky hair that grew in swirling patches from sternum to navel. And beyond. Chantal knew how silky that hair felt, because on occasion, when she had bathed perspiration off his body, she had indulged her whim to touch it caressingly, and not out of necessity.

The memory made her voice husky. "Each Christmas we receive a case of French brandy from a colleague of Father's who has remained a loyal friend."

She stood beside the bed and watched Scout slowly drain the snifter. By the time he was done, he was making a face and punching the pillow beneath his head with his fist. "Here, let me."

She took the snifter from him, then, with one

hand, cupped the back of his head and levered it up. With her free hand she plumped his pillow and turned it over so that it would be cool side up.

It took her by complete surprise when he raised his head a fraction more, enough to bring his face to within touching distance of her breasts. He nuzzled them experimentally, then pressed his face into the V of her shirt and kissed their giving softness.

Chantal moaned and momentarily clutched his head to her. However, she instantly released him and stepped back. Scout appeared to be as stunned by his action as she was. For several ponderous moments they stared at each other. He was the first to speak.

"I don't know . . . I had the strangest sense of déjà vu."

Unaware that she was doing so, she moistened her lips with her tongue and ran her damp palms over her hips. "On the way here," she whispered, "I held your head in my lap."

He lowered his gaze to that region of her body before meeting her wide blue eyes again. "Why?"

"I was afraid you would die."

To ease the thick tension and protect herself from his compelling stare, Chantal reached for the lamp and extinguished the burning wick. "Good night." She turned to leave, but Scout's arm snaked out and caught her hand.

"Chantal?" Reluctantly, she turned back toward the bed. "I didn't follow you away from the party looking for work, you know."

"I know."

"You knew what I wanted."

"Yes."

"What I still want."

In the moonlight she could see that the square patch of towel covering his lower abdomen wasn't adequate to conceal his arousal.

"Don't," she pleaded breathlessly.

"Look, Chantal, this scheme of yours is crazy."

"Not to me. Not to my people."

"Be reasonable. I can't, won't, hang around here to build a damn bridge."

"You will."

He released a long sigh of frustration. "You're an intelligent, educated, refined woman. My Lord, you look like a pagan goddess, a fantasy woman, something out of a dream. Ask me to do something logical, like strengthening the tribe by siring your child. I'd be happy to oblige. But this bridge thing is nuts. You know it is."

"You won't think so tomorrow when you see it."

"Tomorrow I'll be figuring out a way to get away from here and back to civilization."

"We'll see." Her voice held a mysterious inflection as she withdrew her hand from his and rearranged the mosquito netting. She stepped out of the fan of moonlight. "Good night, Scout. You'll sleep very well."

"How the hell do you know how I'll sleep? You didn't—" He sprang into a sitting position. She saw him reel and catch his head in one hand. He cursed viciously and plopped back onto the pillow. "You drugged me again with the brandy, didn't you? Dammit! When will I learn?"

"I'm sorry, but I couldn't stand to see you suffer unnecessarily."

"Then I'm surprised you didn't just shoot me in the head instead of operating on my leg."

"Don't be absurd. I need you too badly to be that wasteful. Good night."

His curses followed her through the otherwise silent house. Eventually, they ceased. The mild sedative, made locally from indigenous berries, had taken effect.

In her room Chantal slipped out of her clothes

and into bed. Usually her room was naturally cooled by the sea breezes. Tonight, though the breezes were blowing, her body remained hot and restless. She was aware of every square inch of her naked skin against the sheets.

She stretched her limbs and arched her back, trying unsuccessfully to relax the taut muscles. She took slow, deep breaths. She folded her hands around her breasts in an attempt to ease the itchy tingling inside them, but that only made her more aware of the tight, sensitive crests. She pressed her thighs together tightly, ashamed of the feverish throbbing between them.

Nothing helped relieve the strange and wonderful symptoms of this physical malady that had afflicted her.

And nothing, not counting sheep, or planning for the bridge, or ritually praying, could rid her mind of Scout's kiss, the feel of his skin beneath her hand, and the sweet pressure of his bearded face against her full, aching breasts.

Five

Chantal was standing beside his bed the following morning as he woke up. For several minutes she enjoyed watching the dappled sunlight play across his features. The lower half of his face was roughly shaded with dark stubble, which was a pleasing complement to his heavy eyebrows. In a day or two he would need a haircut, at least by normal standards he would. She liked the shagginess over his ears and on the nape of his neck.

She watched as the sunlight brought out deep auburn streaks in his normally dark brown hair. There was no gray in it, but she placed his age at around forty, ten or so years older than she.

Or perhaps the network of character lines on his face added years that weren't actually there. In any case, she found the faint creases around his eyes, caused, no doubt, by working outdoors so much, extremely attractive.

He breathed luxuriously and subconsciously laid one hand on his chest, scratching idly as he slowly came awake. His eyes opened, narrowed against the sunlight, then reopened more cautiously. He gave a start when he noticed her and the boy standing at his bedside.

"Who's that?" he asked with sleepy huskiness, nodding toward the lad.

"Jean," she replied, using the French pronunciation. "We call him Johnny."

Scout gave the boy a friendly once-over. "Cute kid. Is he yours?"

"No!"

"No need to get defensive. I was just asking." He smiled at the boy. "Hi there, Johnny. What's happening?"

"*Bonjour, monsieur,*" he said shyly.

"I'm afraid that *Johnny* is the only English word he knows," Chantal informed Scout. "But the two of you should be able to communicate once you get used to each other. For a while he'll be your legs. Just indicate what you want and he'll fetch it for you."

"Can he call me a cab?"

Knowing he was trying to provoke her, she refused to rise to the bait. Rather, she smiled as though he'd made a joke. "Would you like breakfast before or after you shave?"

"Shave?"

She stepped aside, allowing him to see all his toiletries laid out on the nightstand, along with a steaming kettle of water and a basin.

"That's my stuff!" he exclaimed. "Where'd you get it?"

"Out of your trailer at the construction site."

"You broke in and took it?"

"*I* didn't. André volunteered. And he didn't actually break in. The door wasn't locked. I thought you would enjoy having your own things." She indicated the open suitcase on the floor.

Scout acknowledged that, but looked up at her

with shrewd complacence. "The crew will have missed me by now, you know. Everybody has had a chance to sober up after the party. They'll've checked around and noticed I'm gone. They're probably combing the island as we speak, using helicopters, search dogs, everything at their disposal to find me. Sooner or later they'll track me here."

"Search dogs?" she said on a laugh. "Good try, but save your breath. I heard you tell Mr. Reynolds that you were going to lose yourself on the island for an indeterminate time. Nobody, you said, was to come looking for you. Not anytime soon anyway."

His face suffused with hot color. "Add eavesdropping to your list of sins."

"One can't be too careful."

Scowling, he asked, "Did you say something about breakfast?"

"Yes, and you get solid food today."

"For this momentous occasion I really should shave, I suppose. First, however, I need a bathroom." He set his jaw stubbornly. "I'm not going to use that damn bedpan anymore."

"I'm afraid we don't have the plumbing you're accustomed to, but there's a WC of sorts. Johnny will help you get there while I prepare your breakfast tray."

At the door of the room she turned back to him. "Of course you won't do anything dastardly while you're in Johnny's charge, like try to escape. That would place him in an unfavorable light with his family and friends. It would be looked upon as a failure and shadow him the rest of his life."

Johnny, knowing that Chantal was speaking about him but understanding none of it, gazed up at the tall, hairy Caucasian. His guileless, endearing grin revealed that his two front teeth were missing.

Scout smiled back at the boy, then dryly remarked

to Chantal, "While he's around, I promise not to do anything dastardly."

Wearing a pleased smile, she left him with the boy, confident that he wouldn't jeopardize Johnny's standing in the community.

Scout was brawnier than any man in the village. His wound had impaired him, but she had discovered that he was stubborn and would push himself to the point of collapse trying to overcome his temporary handicap. Physically, he could probably still best her. If she were to exercise any control over him, it would have to be psychological.

When she returned bearing the breakfast tray, Scout was scraping off the last of his beard with a disposable razor. His right heel was tucked into his crotch; his injured left leg was dangling over the edge of the bed. Johnny, who was holding a hand mirror for Scout, was sitting cross-legged at the foot of the bed, watching intently. His chin was covered with flecks of white shaving foam.

"But sometimes that mentholated stuff stings. Personally, I prefer the lemon-lime flavor. The fragrance drives the ladies crazy. How's that?" He offered his face up for Johnny's inspection, and the boy eagerly nodded approval. Scout wiped off the remnant foam with a damp towel.

"Okay, let's get you shaved." He turned the razor the wrong way so that the blade didn't actually touch Johnny's skin as he scraped away the shaving foam. "There you are, my man," he said moments later, turning the mirror toward the boy. He giggled with delight.

"I thought the two of you would get along well."

"He's my pal, all right. He helped me get into the first clothes I've had on in days."

Chantal had noticed when she came in that Scout was now wearing a pair of shorts, although he was still shirtless. His chest hair was damp and curly from recent washing. He had combed his hair too. The lemon-lime-scented shaving soap was tantalizing. She caught the clean citrusy scent as she bent to place the bed tray across his lap.

"What's for breakfast? Waffles and sausage?" he asked hopefully. "Eggs and bacon?"

"Rice and fish."

"Huh? For breakfast?"

On the plate she uncovered were two small grilled fish, a bowl of rice, and half of a papaya. After his initial shock, Scout attacked it, wolfing down the food and drinking two cups of coffee in quick succession. He popped the last bite of papaya into Johnny's mouth.

Blotting his lips on a cloth napkin, he looked up at Chantal and asked, "Now what? Not back to bed, I hope."

"Would you like to see the bridge?"

"Yes." His spontaneous answer surprised her, but then he added, pointing his index finger at her, "But only because it's the only way out of here."

She issued Johnny some instructions in rapid French. He scampered off Scout's bed and out of the room. As she had done the night before, she assisted Scout through the house by keeping him propped on her shoulder. When they reached the door to her father's bedroom, she glanced through the door. "Johnny?"

Suddenly, giving a sharp cry, she let go of Scout and rushed toward the boy, who was twirling the pistol off his index finger. "*Mon Dieu,*" she exclaimed, snatching the weapon away from him.

For a moment she held it against her with profound relief, then opened the chamber and shook out the five remaining bullets before stuffing the

gun into the nightstand drawer. Clutching the bullets in her fist, she turned.

Scout was leaning against the doorjamb, glaring
at her from beneath lowered brows. "Sonofabitch,"
he cursed softly.

"I had to lie to you last night," she said defensively. "I couldn't let you lurch for the gun. You
might have opened up your wound."

"I might have escaped by holding you at gunpoint
too."

"That too," she conceded.

She moved to one of the windows, pulled aside the
shutters, and flung the handful of bullets onto the
jagged rocks that led down to the beach below.

"There. The issue of the gun is finished. Done.
There isn't another firearm in the village. With your
leg in the condition it's in, you couldn't negotiate
those rocks in search of the bullets. Forget about
it."

Johnny, who had been cowering against the wall,
approached Chantal hesitantly. He held a wide-
brimmed straw hat which he had been told earlier
to fetch.

As he extended it to her, he whispered contritely,
"Sonofabitch."

She looked at Scout meaningfully. "You'll have to
be more careful of your language, Mr. Ritland." Then
she ruffled the boy's hair. "*Merci*, Johnny." She placed
the straw hat on her head.

When she reached Scout's side, he captured her
jaw in one hand and drew her face up close to his.
"The bullets are irretrievable, so I'll forget about them.
But what I won't forget is how you tricked me. Beware, princess. You'll pay for all your lying."

"No doubt." Defiantly, she yanked her face free of
his grip. "But not before you build my people a
bridge."

Animosity shimmered between them, seemingly on the point of boiling over. Scout believed that had actually happened when, seconds later, a loud rumble reverberated through the village. Throughout the house, glassware tinkled. Doors slammed shut. Books on shelves were shaken loose and fell to the floor. It felt as though a subway train were roaring past beneath their feet.

Scout's anger evaporated. He looked around him with dismay. "What the *hell* is that?"

"Voix de Tonnerre," Chantal replied coolly.

"In English," he bellowed over the ongoing racket.

"Voice of Thunder. Our volcano." His expression registered stark disbelief. She gave a soft laugh of incredulity. "Surely you knew about Voix de Tonnerre."

"Hell, yes, I knew about it. But I didn't think . . ." As suddenly as they had occurred, the sound and vibration ceased. Scout stood with his head cocked expectantly. When he was convinced that the quake was over, he demanded, "Where is it? How close? Is it about to erupt?"

Without her assistance, he hopped toward the front door of the house and out onto the wide veranda that surrounded it on three sides. Johnny raced after him and set Scout's hand on his shoulder. Using the boy as a crutch, he made it down the steps and looked toward the plume of smoke rising above the distant peak.

"Goda'mighty, the thing's about to blow! Chantal, gather everybody together. We'll start evacuating the women and children first. Tell them to bring—"

He broke off when he realized that she was laughing at him. "What's the matter with you?" he asked in a rage. "Have you lost all your marbles? In case you haven't noticed, we've got a live volcano within spitting distance of this village."

"I know, Scout. I grew up with it in my front yard."

"Cute, real cute," he sneered. "You might consider it a friendly neighborhood pet, but molten lava and raining cinders don't sound very friendly to me."

"The lava cools and hardens long before it gets down here, and if there are any cinders in the eruptions, the trade winds blow them out to sea."

"How the hell do you know? You mean you've seen it erupt before?"

"Lots of times. Although it's classified as a nonviolent Hawaiian volcano, it has intermittent, somewhat violent eruptions. They occur every few years. It's been building up to one for the last few weeks. It will come soon."

His disbelief was obvious, and she found it amusing. Nonetheless, she rushed to reassure him. "The eruptions are signals from the gods that they are pleased with the village. The people believe these periodic eruptions are blessings. They look forward to them. You don't see any of them running scared, dashing for cover, do you?"

Scout pivoted like a pogo stick and for the first time noticed that the entire population was standing at the foot of the incline, staring up at them curiously. Everyone seemed to be relaxed. He was the only one on the verge of panic.

"Yeah, well, they probably believe in shrinking heads too," he said, coming back around to face Chantal. "That doesn't convince me it's the thing to do."

Her smile turned to stone. "You don't have to get insulting, Mr. Ritland."

"I'm sorry." In a caustic move he placed his hand over his heart. "I just experienced my first volcanic eruption, so I've got other things besides diplomacy on my mind."

"I assure you that Voix de Tonnerre is harmless."

"What are you, an expert?"

"Yes." Her self-assured retort took him aback. His mouth clicked shut around his next sardonic words. Chantal pressed the advantage. "Father predicts that Voix de Tonnerre won't have any significant eruptions for another thousand years or so."

"Oh, great. Great," he said, rolling his eyes. "Your father says so. Well, why didn't you tell me that in the first place? Now I feel a whole lot better."

"Not only are you insulting, you're sarcastic."

"Well, what makes you think I'd believe anything your father says, huh? I'm convinced he's as mentally unbalanced as you are."

"You can believe him because he's a renowned expert in volcanology," she snapped. "He doesn't operate anything as elaborate as the research laboratory on the slopes of Mt. Kilauea, but I assure you his opinion in these matters carries a lot of weight. So does mine, for that matter.

"And if I'm concerned about a dangerous bridge," she said, warming to her argument, "do you think I'd let my people stay here if I thought the volcano was about to have a violent eruption that could endanger their lives and property?"

He gnawed on the inside of his cheek while he considered what she'd told him. To further convince him, she asked, "I know the Reynolds Group was aware of the volcano. They asked my father's advice before deciding to build their resort on the island. Surely, as one of the designers, you were informed."

"Yes," he said crisply. "I was told I might see a puff of white smoke coming from the crater. I was told it would add to the romantic atmosphere of the island. I didn't expect a drum roll. A damn earthquake. Nothing like what just happened."

"You felt it merely because you're close to it. The

next tremor won't take you so much by surprise. Would you care to see the bridge now?"

He expelled a long breath and ran his hand through his hair in a gesture of frustration and defeat. "By all means. I can hardly wait."

"Watch your step on the path. It's rocky. Rely on Johnny for support. He expects you to."

"I promise not to disappoint him."

Together the trio made slow progress down the path that led into the center of the village. All the smiling people had turned out of the thatched-roof huts to greet them at the bottom of the incline.

As they drew nearer, Scout muttered, "We're conspicuously overdressed. About all anybody else has on is flowers."

The women were wearing skirts of cloth or grass. Around their necks hung garlands of flowers like the traditional Hawaiian leis. The men wore loincloths fashioned of a cotton material, and crowns of flowers on their heads. Few of the children had on anything at all, but all were gaily decorated with enormous colorful blossoms.

"The flowers signify that today is a holiday," Chantal told him.

"What's the occasion?"

She stopped and looked at him from beneath the brim of her hat. "You are."

He, too, stopped in mid-stride on the path. "Me?"

"You're the answer to their prayers. The gods sent you to build a new bridge."

Uncomfortably, he assimilated that. "I thought they'd been Christianized." He nodded toward the hut that obviously served as a chapel. There was a wooden cross affixed to its thatched roof.

"They have been, but ancient tribal traditions are hard to let go of."

"I was hoodwinked, shot, kidnapped, and drugged,"

he reminded her. "Hardly the way to treat a divine being."

"How you got here isn't important. What you're going to do is."

"In other words, what they don't know won't hurt them."

"It's not that. I just see no need to bore them with the details."

As they moved through the crowd, leis were placed around Scout's neck. He was embraced, kissed, touched with awe and reverence. He was adorned, adored, and admired by old and young. Chantal could tell by his dazed expression that the outpouring of affection astonished him. So did the attire of the island women.

"They have faces too, you know," she remarked snidely.

Scout dragged his gaze away from a particularly comely young woman's chest and looked into Chantal's censorious expression. "Forgive me. I'm a victim of my culture. I can't let go my ancient tribal traditions any more than they can. To me a topless girl is still a topless girl."

"After a while you won't even notice."

"Don't bet on it."

Frowning at him with disapproval, Chantal addressed the crowd, which immediately began to disperse.

"Party pooper," Scout muttered.

"They idolize you now, but remember what they expect from you in return."

"A new bridge to replace the old one."

"And there it is."

He followed the direction of Chantal's pointing arm to the deep gorge and the rickety bridge that spanned it.

"Actually, the area we're standing on was formed

when a piece of rock broke off the mountaintop centuries ago," she explained, pointing up at the crest of the mountain on the other side of the gorge. The steep ravine was overgrown with jungle vegetation. At the floor of it, a stream was rushing over rocks and sending up a spray that caught the morning sunlight and threw back hundreds of miniature rainbows.

"That's our fresh-water supply," she told him. "Father dammed the stream to form a small lake. It's around that bend there."

Scout nodded, but he was still staring at the bridge. One of the island men was dragging a balking goat across it. The suspension bridge was swaying precariously. "You carried me across that?" he asked hoarsely. The drop was treacherous. Anyone who fell would be dashed on the rocks far below, he now realized.

"You can see now why I took desperate measures," Chantal said. "Not even the oldest villager can remember when the bridge wasn't there. That indicates that it's at least ninety years old. It must be replaced by a more substantial one."

"I'll grant you that."

"Sit down."

She pointed him to a bench that had been carved out of rock. Johnny dropped to the ground at Scout's feet and stared up at him worshipfully. Chantal stood before Scout as though pleading her case before a stern judge, though he was bedecked with flowers and hardly looked the part.

"If we had a bridge that would support motor vehicles, think what it would mean to the village. The people would have safer, surer, faster access to the rest of the island, to schools and hospitals."

"I see your point, Chantal," he replied reasonably. "Believe me, that thing is a hazard to anybody who gets on it. But what the hell do you want me to do about it?" He spread his hands wide.

"Build another one."

"Just like that?" He snapped his fingers. "Whip it right up? All by myself?"

"Of course not. You've got a free labor force here."

"Here?" Then he barked a short laugh and glanced over his shoulder at the village. "You mean the men of the village?"

"They're not stupid," she said, taking umbrage. "They know the hard work that will be involved and are willing to do it."

"Don't get riled. I didn't mean to put them down, it's just that . . ." He pulled his hand down his face, distorting his features. "There's more to it than picking up a hammer and a sack of nails. If you don't understand that, your father should. And, by the way, why isn't he doing the asking? Why did he delegate this responsibility to you?"

"He and I devised the plan together."

"Even the part about kidnapping me?"

"Yes," she hedged.

"Liar."

"Very well, I added that part. And don't blame the people for any of this. They're innocent. I told them you came willingly but had an accident along the way."

"Look, princess, you don't just kidnap an engineer and, abracadabra, you've got a bridge."

"I'm not asking for another Golden Gate."

"Oh, good, good. For a minute there I was worried."

"All we need is a serviceable bridge."

"To span a gorge that would give an acrophobic nightmares."

"I didn't say it would be easy."

"Grrrahhhh." He threw back his head and released a roar of frustration that only served to blow off steam. It certainly didn't intimidate Chantal, even though it echoed off the mountain slopes and momentarily brought all activity in the village to a stop.

She stood her ground, her chin defiant, her eyes calm. Scout clasped his hands together between his widely spread knees and studied his white knuckles at length.

Finally he raised his head and, in a conciliatory voice, suggested, "Why don't we do this? Why don't I go back to the States and try to raise a bridge-building fund. My . . . uh . . . I've got this friend who's good at raising money for all kinds of charity benefits. It's a hobby with her. She's good at it. Once I explained the situation, she'd hop right on it and give this project top priority. Maybe she could get the Peace Corps or a church organization behind it. Yeah, I'm sure she could. What do you say?"

By the end of his patronizing speech, Chantal was seething. She abhorred his condescending smile and tone of voice, as though he were speaking to a simpleton. She wouldn't even honor his condescension by upbraiding him for it.

Secondly, she didn't want his fiancée in Boston, who she was certain was the "friend" he was referring to, having anything to do with the bridge. Scout wasn't aware that she knew about his Jennifer. For the time being she wanted to keep it that way.

Most infuriating was that he considered the village and its people a charity case. It was that point which she refuted.

"The people want to build the bridge themselves. They don't want the Peace Corps or the Corps of Engineers or anybody else to come in and do it for them. If they did, I would have already asked the U.S. government for assistance.

"They need someone to design it and oversee the construction, but they want to do the actual labor on the bridge themselves. That's the only way they'll consider it truly theirs, something they can take pride in. They don't consider themselves helpless, dimwitted children—which you obviously do."

"I didn't say—"

"Furthermore, we need the bridge here now. You are here now. If we let you go, we'll never see or hear from you again."

He shot to his feet, wincing when he forgot and put weight on his sore leg. "How dare you question my integrity when you've broken your word to me too many damn times to count."

"I never broke my word," she countered with a strong shake of her head.

"Well, remind me from now on to get your word on everything, okay? Because so far you've displayed a tendency toward trickery and downright lying."

"Because I'm desperate!"

"Well, so am I. I'm desperate to get the hell out of here."

"You're refusing?"

"Damn right. I get paid to build bridges and such. Just because you feel a responsibility toward this village, what made you think I would?"

"Common decency."

"Common decency doesn't pay bills. I've struggled for years to make my business a profitable enterprise. Now I've got one of the world's largest conglomerates courting me for my services. I'm not about to pass up that opportunity by staying here and working on your piddling little bridge."

Her blue eyes narrowed dangerously. "Then you're refusing only because we can't pay you. How despicably capitalistic."

Scout raked his fingers through his hair again and blew out a gust of air. "No, it is not just the money. I'm not that big a heel."

"Close."

He fixed her with a hard stare. "Now who's being insulting?"

"Then what, Scout? Why won't you do this for them?" She flung out her hand to encompass the entire village.

"Okay, I'll tell you why," he said, hobbling forward. "Somewhere up there," he said, indicating the foothills she had alluded to earlier, "there's a crazy old Frenchman who sanctions his daughter going around to seduce and kidnap chumps like me at gunpoint. Even thinking about forming an association with a looney-tune like that makes me a little nervous, not to mention that said daughter is also a drug pusher, quack, and liar.

"I've got an active volcano breathing down my neck that could wipe out any bridge I happened to build, which is a crazy, unworkable plan to start with considering the materials and labor force available. Besides all that, I'm having to drink horse broth and eat fish for breakfast and there's a bullet hole in my leg that hurts like bloody hell."

His temper had risen on each word until the last few were issued as shouts that brought a frown of concern to Johnny's attentive face. Chantal, on the other hand, remained impassive, subjecting Scout to an unperturbed, level stare.

Cursing, he glanced away, then brought his gaze back to hers. "Look, Chantal, you're a courageous woman. As a fellow human being, I can appreciate what you've done for the villagers in the past and the way you're looking out for their future. Self-sacrifice like that is rare these days. I admire you for it. I see the need for a new and better bridge, but I'm not the guy you need. You force me to be blunt." He paused to draw a deep breath, then gave her a vapid, sympathetic little smile and concluded with "See, it's really not my problem."

Without a word she turned and casually signaled to the man standing at the end of the bridge. He and several other young men lit the torches they held ready. When each was burning, they held them to the ragged rope. In seconds the ancient hemp and wood was engulfed in flames.

Scout gave a start of outrage and astonishment. Turning to him, Chantal said pleasantly, "*Now* it's your problem."

Six

"Have you lost your mind!" Scout hobbled toward the burning bridge. "I can't believe this," he cried, slapping his hands against his thighs, mindless of his wound. "You're all crazy."

The heat of the fire was intense. It washed over them in visible, shimmering waves. But almost as quickly as it had ignited, it died, having consumed the bridge in less than a minute. Chunks of burning debris floated down into the gorge and fell into the stream, sending up clouds of steam.

A cheer went up from the villagers. To them, the burning of the bridge represented a pledge that they would soon have a new one that wouldn't be life-threatening. They began celebrating in earnest with song and dance. Drums beat out a joyous tattoo.

Scout, impervious to everything except the smoldering remains left at each side of the gorge, came around to confront Chantal. He ripped the flower garlands from his head and neck and tossed them to the ground.

His eyes burned as hot as the flames that had destroyed the bridge. "I'm going to murder you."

Painfully, he began making his way forward. He had spoken with such passion and conviction, Chantal experienced a flurry of fear that he just might do as he threatened.

However, before he reached her, hands aimed for her throat, his arms were caught and pinioned behind his back. "Let go of me," he shouted, furiously whipping his head around.

"Did he hurt you, Chantal?" A muscular young man rushed to Chantal's side while two of his contemporaries, who were just as wiry, held Scout back.

"No, André."

"André." Scout sneered, straining against his captors. "When I get finished with her, I want my chance at you."

"Don't worry," she told André. "He's just a little upset that we burned the bridge and cut off his avenue of escape."

" 'A little upset'?" Scout roared as he struggled with the men who held him. "That doesn't even come close to describing my mood, princess. When I get my hands on you, I'm gonna kill you."

"Do you want me to knock him unconscious again?" André offered.

"No!" she cried, laying a restraining hand on his arm. "Give him a chance to adjust to the idea that he now has no alternative except to build a new bridge."

Scout was closely eyeing André. "Don't I know you?"

"I was on the construction crew for the hotel."

"Yeah, I remember now. You were a good, strong workman, but you had a real attitude problem." He snorted. "No wonder. You were only acting as her lackey and spy."

André lunged at Scout, ready to fight. Again Chantal held him back. To Scout she said, "You would do well to make friends with André. He'll be valuable to you when you start on the bridge."

Scout made an obscene suggestion about her and her bridge. This time Chantal didn't react quickly enough. Before she could stop him, André slugged Scout in the mouth. Scout, strengthened by rage, managed to free his arms. His fist took a swipe at André that clipped him solidly on the chin, splitting skin.

"Stop it!" Chantal stepped between them. "Stop it this instant! Do you want the people to see you fighting? This is a day of celebration. I won't have your stupid male egos ruining it for them. Johnny," she called. The boy rushed to Scout's side and placed the man's hand on his shoulder.

Chantal hitched her chin in the direction of the house on the hill. Scout was fuming, but his face was drawn and pale with pain. Reluctantly, he shared his weight with Johnny and began the climb up the gradual incline to the house.

Chantal started after them. To her surprise, André gripped her arm. He had never touched her before, nor had he ever looked at her through such hard eyes. "He could be dangerous to you. I do not think he should stay in your house."

She pulled her arm free. "He has to. I must tend to his wound. He certainly won't be any use to us if he develops an infection. There's no need to be afraid for me. He snarls, but he doesn't bite."

He didn't respond to her attempt at humor, only stared at her with implacable, obsidian eyes before turning them malevolently on the two struggling up the hill. Then, wordlessly, he turned away, signaling his friends to follow.

Chantal sighed wearily. She and André had never exchanged a cross word. Why now, when she didn't need any more hassles, was he getting his ire up? Wasn't Scout enough to contend with?

By the time she reached the house, he was sitting on the edge of the bed, unwinding his bandage. Johnny was looking on somberly. Chantal issued swift instructions to him, which he rushed to carry out.

She moved Scout's hands away and inspected the incision. "One of the stitches popped during that ridiculous altercation."

"Your lap dog started it."

Johnny returned carrying a decanter of liquor. Chantal poured an inch of it into a drinking glass and extended it to Scout.

"No thanks. I don't want to sleep through the rest of the week."

"It's nothing but brandy. You saw me pour."

"How do I know you haven't laced the whole bottle?"

She tossed back the shot of liquor and swallowed it whole. Pouring another, she extended it to him. He took it and swallowed as boldly as she. "Thanks," he croaked. His tongue came out to explore the bleeding cut on his swelling lip.

"Grown men," Chantal said with derisive reproach, "slugging at each other." She moistened a corner of a washcloth in the basin of water on the nightstand and dabbed his lip with it.

"Ouch, damn! Stop that."

"I need to put something on it."

"Forget it."

"It could get infected."

He reached for the decanter and poured another shot. Before drinking it, he dipped his finger into the glass and spread the alcohol over his bleeding lip. It caused tears to form in his eyes. "Consider it disinfected."

"Very well. I'll have to put in another stitch—"

"You're not getting your hands on me again, Dr. duPont, so put that thought right out of your mind.

I'll bank on my general good health and the regenerative powers of the human body to heal itself."

"You look feverish. Perhaps you should lie down."

"Perhaps you should drop the phony bedside manner and tell me where it is."

"Where what is?"

"The other way out of this village." He plunked down the brandy snifter and struggled to his feet. "Because even you wouldn't do something as crazy as cutting off the only means of getting to the rest of the island."

"I don't know what you—"

He grabbed her shoulders and jerked her forward. Her hands landed on his bare chest. They stood eye to eye, glaring at each other with open animosity. Johnny made a worried, fearful sound that brought them both to their senses.

Chantal, stepping away from the bed, murmured reassuringly to the boy and stroked his cheek. He bade Scout au revoir and left the room.

"I'm waiting," Scout said tightly as soon as Johnny had cleared the doorway.

Chantal removed her straw hat and shook her heavy hair off her back. "There is a path that snakes down the gorge on one side and up it on the other. But it takes a man almost an hour to walk it, not counting the time it takes to cross the stream. With your injury it would take four times that long if you could make it at all. In any case, you don't know where it is. Resign yourself to building another bridge."

He gave her a calculating look. "Or what?" he asked softly.

Taken aback, she repeated his question. "What do you mean, or what?"

"Exactly that." He crooked his hand around the back of her neck and pulled her over him as he fell back onto the pillows. His hands linked behind her waist to hold her sprawled against him.

"The more I think about being stranded here, the better I like the idea," he whispered against her lips. "What man wouldn't think this was paradise? I could take advantage of what you advertised the other night."

Rubbing a hard kiss on her lips, he skimmed his hands over her body, down to the backs of her thighs and up again. "Once you get warmed up, I'll bet you're a real wildcat in the sack. André could probably testify to that. Wasn't jealousy what caused that fight between us? He doesn't like the thought of my going where he's already been, hmm?

" 'Course he doesn't have anything to worry about. Not really. When I get tired of you, I'll give you back to him. Then I'll choose from among the beauties in the village who were fawning over me this morning. I won't have to work another day in my life, won't have to put on a necktie ever again, won't have to fight rush hour traffic."

He pulled her harder and higher against him and curved his hands over her buttocks. "Why should I go to all the trouble of building a bridge when, the more I think about it, princess, the better I like the thought of whiling away my days here like your daddy has, getting fat and lazy."

His smirk was mocking and insulting. At that moment she wanted to drive a knife through his heart. Instead, she nudged his sore thigh with her knee. When he winced reflexively, she extricated herself from his arms and left him lying there.

"You overexerted yourself this morning," she said coldly. "I'll send Johnny in with your lunch. After that, I suggest you rest."

After closing the door behind her, she leaned against it and allowed the threatened tears to form in her eyes. He had hurt her terribly, cut her to the quick, struck her in the most painful way he possibly could. To respond would have provided him useful ammunition. No, she would die before letting him know how cruel he had been.

It was hours later before she reentered his room.

Scout was sitting up in bed, a tablet propped on his bent right knee. He finished what he'd been writing before glancing up. Then he did a double take. Chantal was standing on the threshold of the room, wearing only a bikini.

She didn't see his astonishment because she was experiencing her own. Pieces of wadded-up paper littered the floor like snowballs.

"I'll have Johnny pick them up later," he said, bringing Chantal's eyes around to him.

"What are you doing?"

"Sketching."

"Sketching what?"

He had trouble staying focused on her face as she advanced into the room. Her navel entranced him, so did her thighs, and her breasts which swelled above the bra of her bikini.

"Ideas," he said in a voice as thick and congested as his loins.

She gazed down at the top sheet of the tablet. "It's a bridge," she exclaimed in a whisper.

"Of course it's a bridge. That's what you brought me here to build, isn't it? Or have you changed your mind?"

"No, but obviously you've changed yours." Fixing him with an unfriendly stare, she asked, "Should I be insulted or flattered that you no longer want me as your whore?"

He let out a whoosh of breath, as though she'd rabbit-punched him. "I deserved that, I guess."

"And more."

Setting the tablet and pencil aside, he gazed up at her. "That was anger and frustration talking, Chantal, not me. I'm not usually like that. I . . . I've been under a lot of pressure these last couple of days, right? I was feeling ornery and—"

"Hateful."

"Hateful," he admitted. "I struck out at you where I suspected you might be the most vulnerable."

"Then you're very intuitive, Mr. Ritland, because everything you said, indeed, your entire attitude, was contemptible."

"Back to Mr. Ritland, are we?"

"For the time being."

"Will I win any Brownie points if I show you some ideas? I've been toying with several this afternoon. I had Johnny fetch me this tablet and pencil from George's—you don't mind if I call him George, do you?—study. It's rough, but—"

"Why are you doing this?"

His head snapped up. "I thought you wanted me to."

"I do. But you've capitulated so suddenly. Why?"

She was the most exasperating female he'd ever met. Here he was, trying to be nice, doing what she'd been wanting him to do, and she wanted reasons and explanations.

"Believe it or not, I'm a well-liked guy in most circles," he said. "My business dealings with people have been, on the whole, congenial. I avoid confrontations when at all possible, and until this morning I hadn't engaged in a fistfight since high school," he added, touching the cut on his lip with the tip of his tongue.

"I'm sorry André struck you, although you deserved it for using that kind of language with me."

"I'd been sorely provoked, Chantal," he reminded her softly.

Her voice was equally low. "So what caused you to change your mind?"

"I started feeling selfish. I've had some good fortune lately." He shrugged. "I thought maybe I should spread some of it around. If I can help these people out, I believe I should."

What he didn't tell her was that he had come to the sudden realization that almost a week had passed since the Coral Reef's opening. One week closer to his wedding day.

Jennifer would be expecting him home soon, though he'd never set a specific date for his return. But he knew that if she didn't hear from him within a reasonable period of time, she would get in a tizzy.

She might understand his desire to do some hunting, fishing, and sight-seeing on Parrish Island. But if his excuse for being detained was that he'd been stranded under the same roof in a remote village with a woman who looked like Chantal, it might be a bit much to ask his future bride to dismiss.

In any case, he wasn't going to press his luck. The sooner he built the damn bridge, the sooner he'd get away. His opponent seemed unwilling to compromise. So far she'd outfoxed him. He'd decided that a different strategy was called for.

Now she stood with her arms crossed over her bare stomach, her expression skeptical. "That's very altruistic of you, Mr. Ritland."

"You don't believe me?"

"No," she replied bluntly. "But your reasons for cooperating now aren't as important as getting the bridge built. Would you like to go outside for a while?"

"Don't you want to see what I've got so far, hear my ideas?" Her lack of enthusiasm was perturbing. He had expected gratitude, surprise, anything but her seeming nonchalance.

"Later. I think you need some fresh air. Come on.

I'll call Johnny. Together I think we can get you down to the beach."

It was a painstaking process, but eventually the three of them reached the bottom of the rocky path that led from the back of the house to the beach. Actually, Scout felt he could have gone much farther without complaint. The trek provided him with a valid reason to touch Chantal.

While she supported him on one side, his hand had ridden in the curve of her waist. He didn't know if his dizziness came from lying in bed so long without any exercise, from the hot sun, or from gazing down at Chantal's breasts from the spectacular vantage point he had.

"Sit in this tidal pool. The saltwater will be good for your incision."

He eyed the shallow pool dubiously, but lowered himself into it. As soon as the water covered his leg, he pulled it out. "It's hot. Besides that, it stings."

"Don't be such a whiner," she chided, and pushed his leg back into the water.

The scenery was travel brochure material. The sand was the color and texture of sugar, the water aquamarine. White, foaming waves were driven ashore, then receded, leaving behind a sparkling, lacy residue on the beach. A few men of the village were spear fishing. Women were playing in the surf with their children.

None was wearing anything except a South Seas version of a G-string. None seemed to notice except Scout. But even with such a plethora of nakedness, the person he stared at most was the one who was clothed. He couldn't take his eyes off Chantal as she cavorted in the waves with Johnny and some of the other children.

Emerging from the water, hair slicked back from her exquisite face, droplets of water collecting on her satiny skin, eyes shining with pleasure, she took his breath away and made him painfully aware that it had been a long time since he'd been with a woman. He was glad his lap was partially submerged in the shallow pool.

"How does it feel?" she stunned him by asking as she dropped down onto the sand beside him. "I see it's still swollen a bit."

He cleared his husky throat. "I beg your pardon?"

"Your lip." She touched it experimentally with her cool, damp fingertip.

His stomach muscles contracted sharply. "It's fine."

"And your incision? Is the warm saltwater helping?" She licked seawater off her lips, and his heart seemed to somersault.

"Oh, yeah, the soaking has made it feel a lot better."

"Good. I thought it might." Gathering her hair in her fists and drawing it forward over her shoulder, she wrung water out of it.

"You know," he commented, forcibly pulling his eyes away from the trickles that rolled down her stomach and pooled in the V of her thighs, "I get the distinct impression that I'm this afternoon's entertainment."

"What do you mean?"

"Well, every time somebody looks over here, they start laughing. What's so funny about me? Surely they're accustomed to my hairy chest by now."

Chantal lowered her eyes. He noted how her wet lashes clung together in dark, spiky clusters. "They're not finding you amusing. It's me they're giggling at."

"You? What's funny about you?"

"Not funny. Just different."

"Different?"

She glanced at him briefly, then away. "They're not used to seeing me on the beach . . . uh, wearing a top."

Instantly, his eyes dropped to her breasts. He noted for the first time that the bikini bra looked brand new. The color was a shade more vivid than the bottom. He doubted it had ever been worn.

For such a slender woman, she had full breasts, beautiful breasts. The centers were making distinct impressions against the blue top. He remembered how responsive they had been to his caressing fingertips, and imagined their texture against his gently flicking tongue. The fantasy caused an explosion of hot desire deep in his belly.

"Please don't change any native customs on my account."

Slowly, he lifted his gaze to her eyes, which were as brilliant as the sun on the ocean waters. For several heart-exercising moments, their eyes communicated what their bodies were feeling. Instinctually, he reached out and encircled her wrist. His thumb pressed against the pulse; he wasn't surprised to feel it racing in tempo with his.

"Please?" he added in an undertone.

A soft moan escaped her damp lips, but she pulled her hand away from his loosely shackling fingers. "If you were European, perhaps. But, by your own admission, American men are obsessed with breasts." She made a vague gesture, which was meant to close the discussion. "Why don't you show me your sketches now?"

He willed his body to relax, but obstinately refused to let her off so lightly. Spontaneously, he plucked a hibiscus blossom from the bush behind her. Then, holding her inquisitive stare with his own, he pressed its stem into the valley between her breasts so that the petals spread open upon the smooth mounds.

"Now we'll look at the sketches." His voice was hushed, which surprised him. He hadn't intended to be so taken by his own handiwork. He had in-

tended to unnerve her, but his plan had backfired.
He was the one who was rattled.

Johnny had carried the tablet down to the beach
and anchored it beneath a rock. Scout fumbled with
the rock, but managed to retrieve the tablet. He
smoothed out several sheets of paper.

"I started out thinking about a suspension bridge
similar to the previous one. That, however, involves
cable and supports and, well, it's just not feasible."
He had x-ed through a number of rough sketches.

"The arch bridge," he said, tapping another drawing. "Standard and workable. Unless you happen to
be on an island where the gorge you're bridging is
too steep and there's not an abundance of concrete.
So," he continued, glancing at her as he pointed at
another sheet of sketches, "I fell back on the trestle-
bridge concept. Straight out of a John Wayne western."

"Can you build it here?"

He scratched his head and squinted out over the
ocean. "I don't know. If . . ."

"What?" she asked when he paused.

"If I had the materials." He set aside the tablet and
reached for her hand again. It was a consoling gesture this time. Pressing it between the two of his, he
looked at her and said earnestly, "Chantal, you're
asking me to do the impossible. Even though I've
agreed to stay, even though I've played with several
ideas, I simply can't do it."

Gracefully, she rose and extended him a helping
hand. "Come with me."

"Where?" He was glad to note as he stood up that
soaking his wounded leg had relieved some of the
stiffness and soreness. He still couldn't place much
weight on it, however. Johnny bounded up to his
side. "Thanks, pal. The lady wants us to follow her."
Johnny seemed to understand.

Chantal struck off down the beach. Perplexed,

Scout followed her. She disappeared into a grouping of enormous boulders that sent up sprays of surf as the waves crashed against them. Johnny led him through a shin-deep tidal pool between the rocks.

As they emerged from the crevice on the other side, Chantal was rolling up yards of military camouflage netting. Beneath it were hidden enough building materials to fill a small warehouse. There were sacks of concrete mix stacked in shoulder-high rows so solid they could have served as a bunker, lumber, and every kind of power tool imaginable, even a portable generator to power them. Seemingly miles of steel cable was coiled like huge snakes sunning on the beach. All had been neatly arranged and wrapped in plastic sheeting to protect it from the salt spray.

Scout's mouth dropped open. There was a red logo boldly stamped on all the goods, but even without that he would have recognized the building materials.

"That's . . . you . . ." he stammered. "You're—"

"That's right," Chantal said coolly. "I'm the wily bastard who was stealing from you."

Seven

"How'd you manage it?"

Scout posed the question as he tried to scoop a bite of rice into his mouth from a small bowl. They were eating alfresco on the beach, the breathtaking ocean panorama the backdrop for this ceremonial dinner.

Chantal had warned him that there wouldn't be any silverware. He hadn't thought that would present much of a problem, but his fingers hadn't mastered the skill yet. Most of the rice dropped into his lap.

"I was taught to eat this way before I ever saw a fork or spoon." His futile efforts and exasperation were comical. Chantal laughed at both.

"A person could die of starvation like this."

"Would you like me to give you another lesson?" Setting aside her own food, she licked her fingers clean and turned toward him. "The trick is to hold the bowl close to your mouth and pinch the food up between your fingers. Poke what you can into your mouth and lick off the rest. Like this."

She scooped up a portion of rice and roasted pork

and lifted it toward his mouth. He took the food, then nibbled what remained off her fingers. Chantal watched the movement of his lips and wondered how something so innocent could make her stomach feel weightless. When his tongue brushed the tips of her fingers, she snatched her hand back.

"I think you've got the knack now."

"I wasn't finished practicing."

Her senses reacted to the teasing glint in his eye, but she resisted them. "Try it on your own."

"Thanks for the lesson in table manners à la Parrish Island," he said as he resumed eating, "but when I asked how you'd managed it, I was referring to the stealing."

"Such a harsh word!"

"It carries a harsh sentence if you're caught."

"But I wasn't."

"Until now." His brows were drawn so close together, there was hardly a discernible space between them over the bridge of his nose.

"You're miffed only because you couldn't catch me. The fact that I went undetected bothers you more than the loss of the goods, doesn't it?"

He squared his shoulders and faced her belligerently. "Do you know how much you stiffed the Reynolds Group?"

"No, and I'll bet they don't know either, with the possible exception of a bookkeeper who filed the insurance claim. He could probably tell us right down to the last penny how much the supplies were worth because he was reimbursed that amount by the insurance company."

"So you stiffed them."

"How much do you suppose the Reynolds Group pays in insurance premiums each year? What I took adds up to a tiny fraction of that amount. So everybody comes out ahead."

He was shaking his head with incredulity. "You know what I find most amazing? I think you really believe what you're saying. To you that kind of logic makes sense."

"It does. Perfect sense. Besides, you probably wouldn't have used all those materials. I'm certain you ordered more than you thought you would need. Better that than to run short in the middle of the job, especially since everything has to be brought in by ship. I saved you the expense of shipping the surplus back to the States, and, at the same time, put the materials to good use."

"So, you think it was all right to steal because you needed the materials and we didn't?"

She gasped with affront. "Surely you don't think I'd steal something I didn't need!"

His neck seemed to come unhinged as his head dropped forward until his chin almost touched his chest. "It's like talking to a brick wall."

"Cheer up. Here comes dessert."

The entire population of the village had turned out to celebrate the imminent construction of the new bridge. The villagers seemed to be having a marvelous time, Chantal noted. Everyone except André, who was sitting apart, drinking cup after cup of liquor. Several times during the course of the evening she had caught him eyeing Scout, his expression revealing feelings of resentment and malice.

André was the strongest, and by far the most educated, young man in the village. George duPont had recognized the boy's intelligence and seen to his education at the American school. Though André had hated leaving the village, he had been an excellent pupil.

The duPonts relied on him to do tasks they couldn't

delegate to less sophisticated villagers. He often served as a courier between the village and the people on the far side of the island because he spoke English well and, when necessary, could blend into that culture. He'd been a natural choice to plant at the Coral Reef construction site.

Chantal regretted that André had had a change of heart regarding Scout. It had come about only since the kidnapping. Before then, André had spoken well of the engineer, calling him a tough but fair boss. He had reported back to Chantal and her father that Mr. Ritland was definitely the right person to supervise the construction of their bridge.

It puzzled her now that his opinion of Scout had undergone such a drastic reversal. Scout's theory that André was jealous was preposterous. They had grown up together in the village, had played as children. Never had André indicated any romantic tendencies toward her. Indeed, he could have his pick among the marriageable young women.

This rift between the two men bothered her greatly not only because she loathed disharmony in any arena of her life, but chiefly because the two would have to work closely on the bridge, pulling together, not against each other.

It seemed that all her thoughts eventually came back to the bridge. Scout claimed not to have a definite plan and refused to discuss sketchy ones until he had thought them through. No matter how hard she pressed him, he had remained resolutely silent since discovering that she had been the elusive thief who had plagued the Coral Reef project.

She was eager for the work to commence. What if he left them with an unfinished bridge because he had to return to the States in time for his wedding?

Chantal couldn't detain him indefinitely. As the deadline neared, she would have to confront her conscience and ask for whom she was detaining him, her people or herself. Despite the hostility that frequently flared up between them, she liked having him around.

Looking at him now, she enjoyed watching the firelight from the burning torches flicker across his features and pick up the russet highlights in his hair.

"This is great," he was saying, unabashedly licking the sticky substance off his fingers. "What is it?"

"It's like a pudding. Made with mashed fruit, shredded coconut, and goat's milk."

Abruptly, he stopped eating and glanced sickly down into the shallow bowl his fingers were scraping clean. Laughing, Chantal said, "I shouldn't have told you and ruined your enjoyment. But smile, please. Margot made it for you."

"Who is Margot?"

"Over there. The one anxiously wringing her hands."

He followed Chantal's nod and spotted the girl. Scout held up his empty bowl and rubbed his tummy. The girl's anxiety-ridden face broke into a radiant smile. "How old is she?"

"Eighteen and still unmarried. An old maid."

"She isn't my idea of an old maid," Scout said in obvious appreciation of the girl's Polynesian beauty.

"She's very beautiful," Chantal conceded. "And very choosy. Her parents are nearly frantic to see her married. They want to protect her."

"From what?"

"From men who come to the island from overseas," she said slowly, averting her head. "They usually consider our women a commodity. Girls like

Margot become their prey and are often seduced. When their seducers are finished with them, there's little for them to do except become prostitutes in bars along the harbor and near the military bases."

Scout's happy mood evaporated. "You mean one slip, which is probably not her fault in the first place, and she's ruined for life? That's unfair, isn't it?"

"To these people, a virgin bride is still highly prized."

Voix de Tonnerre chose that instant to belch a geyser of smoke. The night sky was illuminated with a red glow. The earth trembled. A sound like thunder reverberated, echoing off neighboring mountains.

Scout jumped to his feet, forgetting to favor his left leg. A cheer went up from the natives. Drums began beating out a rapid pagan rhythm. Jugs of potent liquor were passed from hand to hand and liberally imbibed.

Scout drank from his own cup as he lowered himself back to the woven grass mat he shared with Chantal. He gestured toward the smoldering crater and the cloud of steam rising from it. "You're sure you know what you're talking about?"

"Positive. My father has studied Voix de Tonnerre all his professional life. We've combined our studies. It's building up to an eruption, but it won't be anything severe or destructive. Trust me. If you find that difficult, trust my father. Few men in the world are regarded as expert as he is."

"And he's up there now? With all that chaos going on? Isn't he frightened of getting trapped when the big blow comes?"

She gazed at the mountain with deference. "He's up there. But no, he isn't frightened of Voix de Tonnerre."

Scout's fingers closed around her chin and brought her head around. His eyes searched her face. "I believe you're half heathen yourself, Chantal duPont."

Her lips curved into a secretive smile. "This culture is seductive, isn't it?"

"It has its perks." He looked down at the bandeau top she was wearing over a short sarong, which rode low on her hips. Between, there was an expanse of smooth, tanned skin that held his attention for so long, Chantal began to feel uncomfortable. "Stop staring at me."

"Belly buttons are among my favorite things," he said huskily.

"You'll really enjoy this part of the celebration, then." She turned his attention away from her midsection and toward a group of young women, including Margot. "They're about to dance for you. Try to appear impressed."

"I don't have to try."

The dancers began moving in time to the beating drums. Their feet sifted through the sand. Thighs flashed in the torchlight. Their gyrating hips defied nature. Smooth bellies rippled with trained muscles that activated the revolving motions of their pelvises.

Baskets of flowers and fruits were lifted above their swinging heads. "They're making an offering to the volcano," Chantal explained.

"I thought the usual practice was to toss in a virgin," he quipped.

"It was." He swung his gaze away from the barebreasted dancing women and looked at her sharply to see if she was teasing. She wasn't. "That was one concession they made when they embraced Christianity."

"Lucky for the virgins," he muttered. Giving the crater a more respectful glance, he saluted it with his drink before taking another sip.

"You're developing a tolerance for our alcohol."

He swirled the contents of his cup. "Not really. Two or three swigs of this and it feels and sounds like a freight train is roaring through my head."

"Then why are you drinking it?"

"Because I'm not as scared of freight trains as I am of volcanoes." He smiled crookedly, and Chantal's heart thudded as vigorously as if she were participating in the dance. When he wasn't scowling or frowning, he had a very nice face. Even when he was scowling or frowning, it was nice, she admitted.

Recently, she had been wondering what her life would have been like if she had met Scout Ritland on the mainland. Would her destiny have been altered? No doubt they would have been attracted. But would they have fallen in love, married, had children?

Fantasies along those lines were too painful to enjoy because she hadn't met him in California. She had met someone else. And even if it had been Scout she had given her innocent love to, the outcome would have probably been no different. The unalterable fact was that in the eyes of the outside world, she was an island girl. Even college degrees and professional acclaim didn't change that.

Suddenly the drums ceased. The resulting silence had an impact that was palpable. The dancers stood like living statues for several moments, leaving their spectators, especially Scout, held in thrall. When they broke their pose, most of them drifted back to their families. A few, however, remained the center of attention.

The occasion seemed to call for hushed tones. Scout leaned close to Chantal and whispered, "What's going on now?"

His breath was as balmy as the sea breeze and felt

good against her skin. The night was exceptionally warm after the volcano's eruption. There was a rivulet of sweat making its way from his temple to his cheekbone.

"They're about to do a different kind of dance. Only the young single girls participate."

"How come?"

"Because the purpose of the dance is to attract an eligible man."

"Oh, yeah? Why aren't you dancing?"

"Because I'm not trying to attract anybody."

His eyes moved over her slowly, coming to rest on her breasts for several moments before meeting her gaze again. "Aren't you?"

Chantal's insides were as hot and unsettled as the simmering magma in the depths of the volcano, but she kept her expression impassive and her eyes cool. "If I were to remove my top and dance in a tribal rite, then you'd know I was trying to attract you."

"That would be a fairly good clue, yeah."

"But I'm not. So don't think of me in sexual terms."

He gave a short, skeptical laugh and lightly poked her navel with the tip of his finger. "Impossible."

Since the drums had started up again, she didn't actually hear the word, but merely read it on his lips. Somehow that made it all the sexier.

She pretended to watch the dancers, but her attention was on Scout. His arm was close to hers and frequently grazed it. She was aware of each time the breeze lifted his hair. Once, several strands of her hair were blown across his face, his lips. He didn't brush them aside.

He commented on the dancers' performance only once by rasping, "Good Lord. They send a message as clear as Western Union."

Margot had moved toward André and was dancing

directly in front of him. Her hips rose and fell and made slow, hypnotic circles that were as beautifully choreographed as they were blatantly carnal. André was watching her through hazy, slitted eyes, his smooth, bare chest rising and falling rapidly.

Arms and legs moved sinuously. Bodies swayed. Breasts and bellies, now glistening with sweat, invited a lover's caress and cooling kiss.

The drumbeats became heavier, faster, louder. They seemed to pass through the listener's body, snipping cords of conscience that would have held one bound to puritanical restraint.

Though Chantal had witnessed this rite since her birth, tonight the drums spoke to her in a new and unique way. She wanted to give her body free rein to do as it wanted, to undulate in response to the evocative rhythm.

Heat swirled in her lower body, begging her hips to rotate in cadence to the drums. Her breasts felt hampered by the bandeau. She craved freedom for them. She wanted to bare them to the sky, the sea, the volcano, the man.

Her head yearned to loll about her shoulders, sending her hair rippling down her back, free and unfettered. Her breath was coming swiftly through her parted lips. She could feel herself slipping into a trance and could barely keep her eyes open. Yielding to the temptation, she let them close as she swayed to the rhythm of the music. Following a crashing crescendo, the drums suddenly fell silent again.

Her eyes popped open. Scout was bending close, staring at her with eyes that reflected the torches and fires burning within himself. His face was shiny with sweat. Drops of it trickled down his neck. His nostrils were slightly flared, and Chantal realized that his breathing was as choppy and fast as her own.

Suddenly he cupped the back of her head and drew it up closer to his. His mouth came down hard on hers. He kissed her fiercely, opening her lips, then thrusting his tongue into her mouth.

His fingers splayed wide on the back of her head. His other hand cradled her jaw and angled her head to one side, allowing him to deepen the kiss. Again and again his tongue entered her mouth. Reflexively, her hands clutched for support. Her fingers curled into the pelt of crinkly chest hair and the taut flesh beneath.

As suddenly as he had moved before, Scout jerked his head back and penetrated her wide, staring eyes with his own.

"It's going to happen," he promised thickly. "You're going to have me inside you." He drew away, putting necessary space between them before they became a public spectacle.

The dance had marked the official conclusion of the celebration. Young men claimed their favorite girl and headed for private spots to do what sweethearts do universally. Families began climbing the rocky slope toward their huts. Torches were extinguished until only moonlight and the rosy glow from the volcano bathed the beach with surrealistic light.

"Johnny?" Chantal called softly.

"Over there." Scout had spotted the boy curled up at the base of a coconut palm, sleeping. "I guess I wore him out today."

"It's a shame we have to wake him."

"Don't." Scout caught her arm before she could take more than one step toward the boy. "Let him sleep. I'll make it."

"Are you sure you can?"

"If you'll help me."

"Of course."

She placed one arm around his waist. He settled his arm upon her shoulders. In this now-familiar manner they began to make halting progress across the beach toward the rocky path that led up to the house.

Between the sandy shore and the incline there was a strip of vegetation. No sooner had they moved into the palm grove than Scout tripped on the undergrowth and went down, dragging Chantal with him. She ended up on her back in a bed of cool green ferns with Scout bending over her.

"Scout," she gasped once she had regained her breath. Her first concern was for his injured leg. "Are you hurt?" His grin alerted her to the truth. "You did that on purpose!"

"Hmm." His lips whisked across hers. She placed her hands on his shoulders and tried to push him off. "Listen," he hissed, trapping her head between his hands, "no matter how many times you deny it, I know you like my kisses. Don't you think a man can feel that, know that instinctively? I know why you tricked me into leaving the party with you, but what we did before you shot me wasn't faked, was it?"

"I—"

"Was it?"

Her will battled her desire. Finally, however, her eyes lowered to his beautifully masculine mouth. Slowly, silently she shook her head no.

Some of the tension ebbed from his body, and he settled against her comfortably. His thumbs took turns stroking her lips. "I didn't think so. You wanted to kiss me then, and you want to now, don't you?"

"Yes," she confessed reluctantly. Then, sliding her fingers up through his hair, she repeated it. "Yes."

Their mouths came together with as much passion as before, but it was a softer, deeper, wetter kiss. Her lips were pliant beneath the firm pressure his applied. His tongue was bold but not invasive as it exchanged stroking caresses with hers.

Finally raising his head, he moaned with hunger and need and buried his face in the hollow of her neck. He formed gentle fists around handfuls of her hair and rubbed it against his cheeks. Chantal arched her throat when his lips went in search of its most vulnerable spots.

Trailing his fingers down her chest, he remarked, "I've never touched skin that felt like yours. It's amazingly smooth."

Deftly, he undid the bandeau and removed it. Chantal, who had so often worn no top, was suddenly suffused with modesty. Scout brushed aside concealing strands of her hair and bared her breasts to the patterned moonlight.

He murmured his appreciation and slid one hand up to cup her breast. "You're gorgeous." He kneaded her, tenderly reshaping the soft mound, then brushed his fingertips across the dusky center and watched it respond.

With each stroke of his fingertips, Chantal's back arched off the bed of crushed ferns. Each caress elicited a strange thrill from her lower body that shimmered in widening circles to the rest of her.

"There's sand on your fingers," she told him in an unsteady whisper.

"I'm sorry. Does it hurt?"

She shook her head. The sand only added another dimension, another texture, to his caresses. His gently plucking fingers raised her nipples to tight, sensitized peaks. With each touch she whimpered in response. Just when she thought he couldn't elevate the level of her desire any higher, he blew on her softly to get rid of the sand.

In her mind she cried his name sharply, but it came out only as a hoarse entreaty. He responded by covering one nipple with his mouth, surrounding it with heat and moisture and fervency and need.

Chantal gripped the supple muscles of his back. Before she realized how it had happened, he was lying between her thighs, rhythmically bumping his hips against hers.

He levered himself up again and took her face between his hands. As he kissed her, the tips of her breasts, still damp from his mouth's caresses, got lost in his wealth of chest hair. They groaned their mutual pleasure.

She lightly scratched his ribs from armpit to waist. Making a low sound, he captured one of her hands and carried it down his body, folding her fingers around the hard ridge behind the front of his shorts.

Chantal gasped, first from shock, then from joy, then from consternation. Did he expect such intimacy from all his lovers? His future wife? Or only from island girls?

She threw him off and rolled from beneath him in one motion. By the time he came to his senses, she was backed against the trunk of a palm, recapturing her breath and covering her breasts with her hair.

"What in hell's the matter with you?" he wheezed, blinking her into focus.

"I had to stop it."

He sucked in deep, dry drafts of air. "Why?"

"Because I don't choose to make love to you."

"You chose to several minutes ago." His voice was tightly controlled, indicating the depth of his rage.

"I'm sorry," she whispered earnestly.

"Sorry won't do this time, Chantal. Sorry won't fix this." He cupped his straining sex for emphasis.

The crude gesture offended her and made her angry. "How dare—"

"How dare you go that far then call it off!" he shouted. "Who do you think you are?"

"Who do *you* think I am?" she retaliated angrily. "An island girl you can use for the duration of your vacation stay?"

"Vacation!" He struggled up to one knee, then to his feet. "You call getting shanghaied and shot and bullied into building a bridge a vacation? After all you've done to me, don't you think I deserve some compensation?"

She crossed her arms over her middle as though he had dealt her a blow. "You expect me to play whore for you while you're building our bridge, is that it? A bridge in exchange for unlimited use of my body?"

That he could have so little regard for her pierced her to the core. It also sorely disappointed her. She had begun to think he was of a higher caliber than most men she had met.

"Very well, Mr. Ritland," she agreed dejectedly. "If it will get my people their bridge, I'll sleep with you while you're here. But," she added, pausing to draw a ragged breath, "you'll know each time you enter my body that that's the only reason I'm allowing it. I'll hate and despise you. And because I truly believe that you are a man of integrity, I believe you'll hate and despise yourself afterward."

She faced him defiantly. "Is that what you want? A whore who regards you no more highly than you regard her?"

He released a long, whistling breath through his teeth, then snarled, "Get the hell away from me before I take you up on your *generous* offer."

She didn't realize how tensely she had been waiting for his answer, or just how important it was to her, until he gave it. Gradually, she relaxed her rigid stance. She moved forward with her arms extended. "I'll help you to the house."

He staved her off. "I said for you to get the hell away from me."

"You'll never make it up the path with your leg—"

"My leg," he interrupted, enunciating the words, "is the least of my problems."

They exchanged a hot, tortured stare, then Chantal turned and scrambled up the path alone.

Eight

Chantal was brewing coffee in the kitchen of her house the following morning when Scout appeared in the doorway. He was propped on a makeshift crutch. She noticed immediately that he had removed the bandage from around his thigh. The scar was an uneven vivid pink line, but the swelling had gone down considerably. His hair was tousled, his safari shorts rumpled. Since he hadn't yet shaved and had obviously slept on the beach, he looked disreputable and mean.

He also looked wonderfully male and endearingly cantankerous. Chantal wondered how she had resisted making love to him the night before.

"Coffee ready yet?" he asked gruffly.

"Almost." She smiled at the boy who was sticking as close as a shadow to the man. *"Bonjour, Jean."*

"Bonjour," he replied sleepily.

She turned back to the wood-burning stove and checked the boiling contents of the speckled blue enamel pot. It would have looked more appropriate in a cabin on the American frontier and was quite a contrast to the fine bone china her father had brought with him from France.

She poured coffee into one of the priceless cups while Scout struggled to lower himself into the chair. She refrained from offering him assistance, guessing that he wouldn't welcome it. As soon as his bottom made contact with the seat of the chair, Johnny propped the crutch against the table, within Scout's easy reach.

"Where did you get that?" Chantal asked as she joined him at the table with her own cup of coffee.

"I made it this morning. *Early* this morning. Johnny brought me a knife when I finally got across what I wanted. He helped me locate a good stout stick." He smiled at the boy, who beamed a toothless grin back at him, sensing his idol's approval.

"It should come in handy."

Scout, nodding, sipped his coffee. Neither was looking at the other directly. Each was thinking of the night before, of the kisses that had been given and received and the caresses that had made them feverish and weak.

To break a strained silence, Chantal asked, "Would you like breakfast now?"

"Not if it means having fish again."

"Everyone got a share of the pig that was roasted for the celebration last night."

"The island's version of ham and bacon?"

She gave a half smile. "I guess so."

"No thanks. I'm really not all that hungry. Coffee's fine. Maybe some fruit later."

She acknowledged with a nod of her head. The tension was killing her. It was difficult to make conversation, but even idle chatter was better than having to endure the silence.

"I see that the stitches of your incision have been removed."

"I took them out myself." That much was obvious.
She waited for him to elaborate. He gave a negligent
shrug. "I didn't, uh, sleep very well and woke up as
soon as it got light. I didn't have anything else to do,
so I took them out."

"Are you sure it was time for them to come out?"

"No."

"Does it hurt?"

"No."

"You grimace when you move."

"It's just damned inconvenient."

"Yes, I'm sure it is. I'm sorry."

"So you've said."

Another awkward silence descended on them. She
used it to refresh their coffee, though neither cup
was empty. As she started to turn away from the
table, Scout closed his fingers around her wrist.

"I never considered you a whore, Chantal."

Through the steam rising from the enamel coffee-
pot, they stared into each other's eyes. When the pot
became so heavy her arm began to ache, she returned it to the stove and sat down opposite him
again and for several moments gazed into the dark
brew in her cup.

"Chantal?" She raised her head. "How could you
think that I regarded you with such disrespect?" he
asked softly.

"You said I kissed like an expensive whore."

"Your kisses are deep, passionate, delicious. Some
women would have been flattered by the comparison."

"Not me."

Daunted for a moment, he stared into his own
cup. Then he looked across the table at her and
said, "You're not telling me everything. Talk to me."

Almost shyly, she looked away before she began
speaking. "I'm the product of three cultures. Polynesian from my mother, French from my father, Amer-

ican from attending school. I knew what to expect when I went to America because I'd seen the speculative glances people gave me on the military base. It's rather obvious that I have mixed blood."

"You're also very beautiful in a rare and unique way. Those glances you interpreted as prejudicial were probably stares of admiration or awe."

"Thank you. Perhaps some of them were, but I learned to be wary. What people don't understand, they usually want to keep at arm's length. If I was admired, it was from afar."

"And when someone got close?"

"Typically, he expected me to be something I'm not."

"What happened when you enrolled at UCLA? Did you date?"

"Yes," she answered guardedly, "but I developed a reputation for being unfriendly and aloof. Actually, I was only being very careful." She left her chair and moved to one of the windows, opening the shutters to allow the fresh morning breeze inside.

"During my senior year there I met a graduate student in the geology department. His name was Patrick. Our dates turned into more than just fun outings."

"You, uh, you fell in love?"

Scout's guess was tentative, but she provided an unequivocal answer. "Very much in love. Head over heels. All the clichés apply. We drifted in a pink haze of happiness. Life was wonderful, our future bright. We planned to get married."

Scout cleared his throat and fidgeted uncomfortably in his chair. Johnny looked at him anxiously, but Scout shook his head to reassure the boy that his discomfort didn't stem from his wound. He couldn't account for it himself, except that he found it damned disagreeable to hear Chantal talking about her love for another man.

Snidely, he asked, "So what happened to Patrick and this pink haze of happiness?"

"He took me to meet his parents." Chantal returned to her chair. Her sleek black brows were pulled into a frown, testifying to her degree of anguish. A soft laugh broke through her lips, but it was a hollow and bitter sound.

"Apparently, when Patrick told them about me, they were charmed by the idea of having a daughter-in-law with such a quaint French name. He hadn't told them that I was only half French." She rolled her lips inward in an effort to screen their trembling. The memory of that evening always made her want to weep with humiliation.

"That was the longest dinner I've ever had to sit through. They were subtle, but I could sense their disapproval and abject horror. There was no scene, no breach of etiquette, just a distinct chill in the air."

Even now she could see the dismay that had come over Patrick's mother's face when she eagerly opened the door and first beheld her son's choice of bride. Chantal had worn her best dress. She had been impeccably groomed. It didn't seem to matter that she had been on the dean's list every semester of her college career or that she was fluent in three languages, including a regional Polynesian dialect. If she had had a horn growing out of her forehead, her fiancé's mother couldn't have looked more stricken.

She wasn't a cruel woman. She would have taken umbrage at being deemed a bigot. No doubt she shuddered at the very thought of the Ku Klux Klan or the neo-Nazis. Yet it was unthinkable that her nice WASP son planned to marry a woman of mixed heritage.

"Patrick broke off our engagement two weeks later," she concluded in a quiet, introspective voice.

"Gutless wonder."

"Tremendous pressure was placed on him."

"Why didn't he just tell his folks to bug off?"

Chantal strived to remain calm. Scout was only asking questions she had asked herself a thousand times, but somehow hearing them from him provoked her. "His parents' disapproval wasn't his only reason. There were other factors involved."

"Like what?"

"Like children."

"What about them?"

"He didn't feel that we should have any."

"Why not?"

"He didn't think it would be fair to impose a stigma on them."

"*Stigma?* Your being their mother would be a stigma?"

"You're putting words in my mouth."

"And you're defending this creep, for chrissake." Raising his voice, Scout thumped the table with his fist hard enough to make the china rattle. "To hear you, you'd think you were still in love with him."

"I'm not!"

"Well, good!" The shouting match ended abruptly. Scout combed his hair for the first time that morning, using ten frustrated fingers. They did more damage than good.

"Believe me, Chantal, you're better off without a jerk like that. He sounds like a real loser. He wouldn't have been the husband for you. Be glad the physical commitment—" He broke off when he read her stark expression. "Oh. He got the goodies first and then left you holding the bag."

Her steady gaze turned as blue and cold and

hard as a diamond. "Patrick wasn't so different from most men."

Scout flopped back against the slats of his chair and flung his arms out to his sides. "Oh, I get it now. You shoot—literally, in my case—all the dogs because one mangy mongrel had fleas."

"Interesting choice of words. Patrick wasn't the mongrel. I was."

"You know what I mean," he said impatiently. "He didn't mind sleeping with you but threw you over because he couldn't take the heat from his parents. So now every time you meet a Caucasian man, your built-in security system goes off."

"Wouldn't yours?"

"Not if I was sure of myself."

"I am. It's other people I'm not sure of. Until I know that I'm wholly accepted for what I am—"

"You aren't going to put out for any guy who comes on to you."

"You could use some finesse, Mr. Ritland."

"And you could use some trust. Have I ever treated you disrespectfully, like I thought you were a lesser being because your mother happened to be Polynesian?"

"Yes!"

He was flabbergasted. "That's a damn lie! When?"

" 'If I get captured by a lovely, bare-breasted native girl, don't come looking for me anytime soon.' " Having his own words to Corey Reynolds repeated, caught Scout off guard. His jaw dropped open, then snapped quickly shut.

Chantal took advantage of his speechlessness. "I take that to mean that as long as a 'native girl' is entertaining you, you are willing to stay lost. Implying, of course, that a girl from Parrish Island is amoral and promiscuous, willing to 'put out' for any man for as long as he wants her." She paused to draw a deep breath. "I'm sorry, but I won't be your native girl."

Scout had recovered from his embarrassment. Now he gave an exaggerated groan of irritation. "Give me a break, will you? That was a figure of speech, Chantal. Two men spouting off, the way guys do about women."

"Well, I didn't appreciate it, either as a native girl or as a woman."

Cursing, he threw up his hands in a gesture of surrender. "All right. I apologize. The comment wasn't intended to be overheard. It was insensitive. I'll forgive you for eavesdropping if you'll forgive me for being a slimy, chauvinistic jerk, okay?"

"Now you're making fun of me. In addition to thinking me fair game, you consider me stupid."

Both his hands hit the table at the same time, making a loud slapping sound. "Hasn't it occurred to you that I might have been coming on to you for very basic, honest reasons? Like because I think you're beautiful? Because you're unique and because there's an aura of mystery surrounding you that I find as sexy as hell?"

He reached for her hand across the table and massaged the palm with the pad of his thumb. "I haven't wanted to kiss you since the minute I laid eyes on you because of or in spite of who your parents are, but because you've got one of the most enticing mouths I've ever seen. You've got skin that feels like a flower petal, hair as dark as midnight, and eyes like bottomless lagoons. In case you think I'm just waxing poetic to win you over, I'll throw in something brazen and sexist like this."

He leaned forward and, drawing her hand toward him, pressed it against his chest. "I've fantasized a lot about having you naked and hot and moving beneath me, taking all of me inside your lovely body."

Her lips separated, partly from surprise, partly from arousal. Slowly, she released the breath she had been holding for so long she couldn't recall the last time she had exhaled.

"You shouldn't say things like that to me, Scout."

"Why not? I think you should know how I feel. I want you to know why I desire you. It's not because you're convenient. It's not because I think you're easy. For pity's sake," he said, laughing huskily, "I've endured tremendous hardships for you. How could I consider you easy?" Squeezing her hand tightly, he asked earnestly, "Why don't you believe me?"

It took some tugging but she finally managed to withdraw her hand from his. She stared at the imprint his fingers had left on hers, then slowly looked into his eyes. "Because of your fiancée."

Nine

"Jennifer?" Scout asked weakly.

"I believe that's her name, yes."

Giving no outward sign of her distress, Chantal got up and carried their cups and saucers to the dry sink and pumped water over them.

"I guess if you overheard everything else Reynolds and I talked about, it stands to reason that you heard about Jennifer too."

Mustering her courage, she turned to confront him. "Your wedding date is fast approaching, and Miss Colfax is a lovely young woman who dabbles in antiques."

"Look, Chantal—"

"Never mind, Scout," she said wearily. "Please don't insult my intelligence with needless explanations. And don't involve me in your two-timing. I won't be a temporary diversion until you return to your blushing Boston bride."

He had the grace to look abashed, a man caught red-handed trying to get away with the oldest trick in the book. "I never meant to insult or compromise you, Chantal. I honestly haven't been thinking much about my marriage or Jennifer. Certainly not last night."

"Do you expect me to believe that?"

He ducked his head ruefully. "No, I don't expect you to believe it. But it happens to be the truth."

"That doesn't speak well of either of us, does it?"

"No," he admitted. "Especially of me."

"We were both at fault. I wasn't thinking about her either, Scout," she confessed softly.

His head came up and their gazes locked again. A ponderous silence filled the kitchen, but the village was beginning to wake up. There were sounds of ordinary daily activity coming from the bottom of the hill. The familiar noises seemed remote and far away; in their fog of desire and guilt, Chantal and Scout couldn't be distracted by those sounds.

Suddenly Johnny's stomach growled loudly. Snapping to, Chantal spoke to him in sibilant French and, after silently consulting with Scout and being granted his permission, he left in quest of breakfast.

"Despite everything else I've done, I wouldn't keep you from your wedding," she told Scout. "So work needs to commence as soon as possible. Unless, of course, you refuse to build our bridge now that you know I won't be sharing your bed."

"I said I would do it and I will," he said with asperity.

A knot of apprehension inside her chest began to unravel, although she kept her relief a secret from him. "Are you prepared to show me some designs now?"

"Before I do, I want to know the truth."

"About what?"

"Boats."

"Boats?"

"As I was sitting on the beach this morning, I

contemplated an escape by sea. I didn't see any ships on the horizon that I might flag down."

"The shipping channel runs along the opposite side of the island."

"I thought as much," he grumbled. "When Johnny finally understood what I was asking him about, he became so distressed I didn't have the heart to press."

"The village has numerous boats that are used for fishing. They were hidden from you, but more for your sake than for ours. I was afraid you might try something stupid." He gave her a wry look but said nothing.

"Rarely are these small boats taken to the other side of the island because the currents between here and there are treacherous. Even the most expert rowers find it a challenge. One man couldn't do it alone. It would take a motorboat, and we don't have one."

"How did you get those building materials here? Not by fishing canoe."

"We borrowed a small transport ship that was in dry dock."

"Borrowed? From . . . never mind. I don't want to know."

"Well, the navy wasn't using it, and we put it back right where we found it."

Shaking his head, he chuckled. "You've gotta be telling the truth. Who would make up such a tale?" He studied her face at length, his expression a mix of incredulity and admiration. "Sit down, Dr. du-Pont."

After a brief hesitation she slid into the chair across from him again. She was afraid that the furrow between his brows portended bad news, but she waited to hear him out.

"You're not going to like this." Dragging his hands down his unshaven face, he muttered, "God knows what you'll read into it since it follows our discussion about my upcoming wedding. Believe me, Chantal, that didn't enter into my thinking when I devised this alternative."

"Alternative?"

"Don't jump to conclusions," he said, sensing her suspicion. He fished in the pocket of his shorts and withdrew several sheets of notepaper which, according to the creases that criss-crossed them, had been folded several times. "I've devised a workable way to get from one side of the gorge to the other. At least it works in theory."

"Then why don't you think I'll like it?"

"Because it requires making some compromises. As I've learned, making compromises isn't your strong suit."

She clasped her hands on the table. "What is your idea? I'm not as unbendable as you assume."

"Okay." He spread the sheets on the table. Chantal noticed how strong his hands appeared. Tanned. The backs sprinkled with sun-bleached brown hair. A workingman's hands, callused at the tips, the nails blunt and square and clean.

Unwillingly, her mind entertained memories of those hands moving over her skin, caressing her body, remolding it to fit his palms, using his fingertips to bring her such erotic pleasure she thought her heart would burst.

When he returned to Boston and his Jennifer, would she regret not making love with him when she had had the chance?

"—without difficulty."

"I'm sorry," she said, snatching her attention back to him, "what were you saying?" He looked at her strangely. Defensively, she lashed out, "I can't make head or tail out of this." She gestured impatiently to his crude drawings.

"Then scoot around here so you can see the drawings from the same perspective that I have."

As he had suggested, she moved her chair around the table and set it close to his. Her leg brushed his when she sat down, but she studiously pretended not to notice the contact.

"What are all those little slashes?" she asked, pointing to the series of pencil marks he'd made on the paper.

"As I was saying while you were obviously woolgathering, building a bridge isn't feasible, unless you want to start braiding hemp and put up one like the one you just torched."

"What? Yesterday you were talking about trestles and arches and—"

"Wait a minute. Let me explain, will you?" She fell silent. He took a deep breath and resumed. "I'll build a suspension bridge, but it won't be on the same latitude that the old bridge was. It will be much lower, down here where the gorge tapers to a V," he said, making a mark an inch above a squiggly line which she assumed correctly designated the stream. "It might be, oh, thirty, forty feet across at that point."

"I don't understand. How would anyone get down to it?"

"That's what the dashes are. They represent a series of concrete steps built into the ravine."

"Steps that lead down to the bridge," she mused out loud. "A shorter bridge, easier to build, that wouldn't require so many materials."

"Or so much manpower."

"Or so much time." Her eloquent eyes softly collided with his before moving down to the sketches again. "How steep would these steps be?"

"If they went straight down, they'd be very steep. That's why I've zigzagged them. They won't be nearly as steep as the gorge itself. It would probably keep a crew of workers constantly busy to keep the jungle from covering them."

"That would be no problem. You mentioned compromises."

He scratched his head. "For one thing, it would take an average pedestrian longer to get across the gorge than it previously has. It would also be an aerobic exercise."

"But it would be much safer than crossing the old bridge."

"A trade-off there to be sure."

"What else?" she asked.

"Nobody infirm could get across."

"Nobody infirm can cross the one we have."

"*Had.*" He glanced up at her and smiled.

"Had," she repeated softly, then cited another disadvantage to his plan. "And the village would still be inaccessible to motor vehicles."

He tossed down his pencil and released a heavy sigh. "That's the biggest hangup, Chantal. I spent most of the night trying to figure out a way to construct a serviceable bridge with the limited resources at my disposal. There just isn't a way. I'm sorry I'm not a miracle worker. I can't span that wide a gorge without landmovers, cranes, modern materials, and months of hard work by a crew of experienced engineers.

"The men of your village, willing though they might be, aren't skilled laborers. That's not a put-down. It's a fact. I think I can build you a pedestrian suspension bridge near the bottom of the ravine, one supported by concrete pillars and steel cable, but that's the best I can do."

She studied his face and earnest expression. It appeared to be baldly honest. Not a trace of deceit was apparent. In fact, he seemed genuinely sorry that he couldn't make her a better offer.

"All I ever asked for was your best, Scout."

He gave her a slow smile. "Then you want me to proceed with this plan?"

She stood and pushed up the sleeves of her shirt. "By all means. Where do we start?"

He came out of his chair slowly and with effort. Settling his armpit in the crook of the handmade crutch, he said, "Assemble the troops, princess. Your commander in chief is about to address them."

"When did you start wearing glasses?"

From across the living room Scout had been watching Chantal for some time. The room was lighted only by oil lamps placed on end tables. They cast shadows across her face, which was intent with concentration. She had several lava rocks lined up in front of her on a low table and was making notations in a journal.

Glancing up, she peered at him through the lenses of her eyeglasses. "Since high school. Only to read."

"Hmm. What are you working on?"

"Data on Voix de Tonnerre."

"What for?"

She didn't answer him. Instead, she propped the glasses on the top of her head and looked at him with concern. "You seem tired, Scout."

"I am."

"Why don't you go to bed?"

"Too much on my mind."

She had been sitting with one foot tucked beneath her. Now she set her notebook aside, left the sofa, and moved toward him, her bare feet soundless on the floor. "My father says I give terrific neck rubs. Maybe that will help relax you."

"Sounds great." She moved behind his chair and began to massage his neck and shoulders with skillful hands. It felt wonderful, but Scout didn't believe it would relax him. Around Chantal he never felt relaxed.

More than a week had passed since the night of the celebration and their unconsummated lovemaking on the beach. He was still keyed up and edgy. He seemed to be running a low-grade fever that he couldn't shake. He'd been popping aspirin tablets every few hours, but the fever persisted.

"It's been hotter the last few days than when I first got here, hasn't it?"

"It's the volcano," she explained as she squeezed the tense muscles between her fingers. "The two eruptions today warmed up the atmosphere."

So did looking at Chantal. Every morning she dressed in unglamorous shirts and shorts and joined the work crews. But her breasts did a lot for the shirts, and what her long, bare legs did for the shorts kept him as close to eruption as Voix de Tonnerre. Even when she was wearing heavy boots and thick socks her legs looked graceful.

To shade her face, she constantly wore the wide-brimmed, battered straw hat. It was ugly, but when he had teased her about it, she reacted strangely and assumed a wounded expression. He figured it held a sentimental value to her. Anyway, he was coming to like the damned thing and often found himself looking for it among the workers lined up on either side of the steep gorge.

The evenings were quiet. They shared the shadowed rooms of the house. For the first several days he often reached for a light switch whenever he entered or exited a room. Now he barely noticed the absence of electricity. There was a battery-powered radio in George's office. They listened to a news station for half an hour after dinner to get the news of the day, but all the happenings in the world seemed of little or no consequence to the island village.

Oddly, Scout didn't miss television, his VCR, or any of the other assorted electronic toys he had back home. He was content to spend the evenings reading through the duPonts' vast personal library, or simply watching Chantal while she studied geological charts that looked like Greek to him.

The pictures were another mystery.

On the second day of construction, while the village men were transporting materials from their hiding place on the beach to the work site, Scout noticed Chantal taking a well-camouflaged path up the other side of the ravine.

"Where the hell's she going?" he asked Johnny rhetorically.

He didn't expect an answer, but the boy, having spotted Chantal before she disappeared through the jungle foliage, began speaking. "What? Slow down, slow down," Scout said, trying to make some sense of the boy's French.

"*Photographie.*"

"*Photographie?* Photograph? She's taking photographs?"

"*Oui, oui,*" the boy said excitedly, pleased that he'd made himself understood. He pantomimed looking through a camera and snapping the picture.

"Photographs," Scout muttered, shaking his head in consternation. "Of what?"

Chantal returned several hours later. Scout saw her pass a canister of undeveloped film to André. The man listened to her instructions, then disappeared himself.

"Whose camera?" he had asked as he entered the house, surprising her as she removed it from around her neck.

"My . . . my father's."

His crutch thumped across the floor. He picked up the camera and turned it end over end, examining it assessingly. "Pretty snazzy."

"It's very intricate, yes."

"Where have you been with it?"

"In the foothills."

"To see your father?"

"Yes."

"To take pictures of him?" She made a face which indicated that was the silliest question she'd ever had posed to her. "Okay, I give up. What are you taking pictures of?"

"The volcano."

"Ah. And you sent André to have the film developed."

"What's wrong with that?"

"Nothing. Just wondering. How is George?"

"The same."

"What's he doing up there? Isn't he the least bit curious about everything that's going on down here? Doesn't he want to know how we're solving the problem of the bridge? When am I going to have the pleasure of meeting him?"

She had taken off her hat and was using it to fan herself. "I'll show you the photographs as soon as I get them back. I think you'll find them fascinating. But now you'll have to excuse me. I'm very hot and want to wash off."

He hadn't needed her to tell him that she was hot. He had already noticed. Perspiration had made her shirt stick to her skin. A bead of it was inching down her throat. He wanted to catch it on his tongue. The dark centers of her breasts were discernible beneath the patch pockets of her shirt. Scout had had a hell of a time keeping his eyes off her chest.

The subject of the photographs and her father had been suspended. He hadn't thought of it again until now. "Did the pictures turn out?" He felt her hands pause on his shoulders. "The ones you took the other day."

"Oh, yes, they came out very well. Would you like to see them?"

"Some other time. Don't stop what you're doing. Don't ever stop."

Laughing softly, she laid one hand across his forehead while she slid the fingers of the other up his neck and through his hair to massage his scalp. He emitted a low, satisfied sound. "No wonder George highly recommends your neck rubs. That feels great." She continued to massage his scalp and neck. "How does your *papa* feel about your sharing a house with a man while he's away?"

"He's French, after all."

"What did he think of your affair with Patrick?"

She shrugged. "How does a father usually feel about his daughter's love affairs? His emotions were mixed."

"So you told him everything, even the reason for the breakup?" In order to address her face-to-face, he angled his head back. The crown of it dug into her stomach. His question had caused her uneasiness. He could see it in her eyes.

"No. I didn't tell him about that."

"Your father is the reason you let Patrick off so lightly, right?"

"I don't know what you mean."

"Oh, yes, you do." He grasped her hands when she would have moved away. "You saw how heartbreaking it was for your father to be alienated from his family and friends, even his country, when he married your mother. You didn't want that to happen to good ol' Patrick baby."

Scout felt an intense dislike for the Californian he had never met. He envisioned him as bookish and effete with slightly stooped shoulders and soft, skinny hands the color of old putty. Each time he thought about Patrick's hands moving over Chantal's skin in a lover's caress he wanted to hit something. Hard.

He had always considered jealousy of any kind stupid in the extreme. Jealousy for a man he had never even met was ridiculous. Nevertheless, the green-eyed monster had him by the throat and was choking him.

"I didn't want Patrick to feel obligated to me, so I released him from the engagement without a fuss." Her tone was haughty. "I made up my own mind about it. I don't throw temper tantrums when I don't get my way or when something I want is taken away from me. I'm a grown woman."

His eyes were on a level with her breasts, which were rising and falling with agitation. "So I've noticed."

Beneath his shorts he was full and firm. Being semi-hard all the time, with no relief, was beginning to get on his nerves and make him irritable. He couldn't control his body's biological reaction to Chantal any better than he could control his juvenile jealousy of Patrick. That irritability caused him to speak snidely now.

"You enjoy making me crazy, don't you?"

"I find this topic tiresome, Scout. Let go of my arm."

He did, but he rose from his chair and hobbled after her when she moved into her bedroom. She went to a vanity table that was French in design and more feminine than any other piece of furniture in the house. When he had first commented on it, she'd told him that George had had it shipped from France for Lili. Chantal had inherited it when her mother died.

The room was lit with candles. They spread a

warm glow, a warmth missing in her voice. "I'd like to go to bed now."

"So would I."

"Scout, please. I thought we had this settled."

"Settled?" He laughed scoffingly. "*Settled* hardly describes my current physical state." He braced his hands on either side of the doorjamb to help take the pressure off his left leg. "What would you do if I ignored your protests, came to you now, and started kissing you?"

"You wouldn't."

"Don't be so sure." The sinister undertone in his voice surprised even him, but his frustration was such that he excused it. He hadn't touched her, but he hadn't forgotten what it felt like. He wanted her more than ever.

Jennifer, who was touted as a beauty, was becoming a more dim memory with each passing day. She would be planning parties, receptions, heaven knew what in preparation for their wedding. She was spoiled rotten and could be a real pain, but she didn't deserve to have her fiancé lusting after another woman with every cell in his body, tossing and turning nightly in a pool of his own sweat because of the fantasies he was helpless not to envision.

He'd never been like this before. Was it Chantal? Or was it the situation? The setting? Was she seductive simply because the scenery was and she was in the center of it?

One sleepless night he had toyed with that rationalization for about a second and a half before trashing it. If Chantal duPont had crossed his path anywhere in the world, she would have had the same stupefying effect on him.

He was almost forty years old. His love life hadn't been the stuff legends were made of, but he had been involved with enough women to make fair comparisons. Nothing he had experienced before compared to the engulfing, maddening, saturating desire he felt for this woman.

It was more than lust. He wanted inside her body, yes, but he also wanted inside her head. She was the most intriguing individual he had ever met. He wanted to probe behind those blue eyes until he knew intimately the mind and soul of the woman they mirrored.

Watching her now, he saw a spark of apprehension in those gorgeous eyes. Cursing beneath his breath, he relaxed his arms. They dropped to his sides. "I wouldn't start kissing you," he said hoarsely. "I don't fancy dying by poison dart, machete, or fishing spear."

"What are you talking about?"

"Your watchdog. André. He resents like hell that I'm here in this house with you night after night. I wouldn't be surprised if he were camped outside in the dark under a palm tree waiting for you to scream for help."

She dismissed his hypothesis with a small shake of her head. "He obeys your orders on the job."

"Resentfully. He does what he's told only because you've asked him to and because he knows I'm doing something good for the village. He doesn't like taking orders from me. Looking back, I realize that he never did. Even on the Coral Reef job, I was on the receiving end of some bad vibes. And now," he added, "I know why. From the beginning he considered me a threat, a competitor for your affections."

"That's ridiculous."

"Tell that to André. He considers you his and would welcome the chance to throttle me. If I were to step out of line, he'd kill me and ask questions later."

She was the very essence of woman: soft but strong,

straightforward but mysterious, simple but complex, elegant but sexy.

His smoldering stare made her self-conscious. He saw her swallow and nervously moisten her lips. From out of the shadows her voice came to him husky and unsure. "What?"

"Nothing," he replied as he turned to leave. "I was just thinking that you might be worth dying for."

Ten

Chantal spotted him as he came huffing down the hill toward the beach. Even from a distance she could tell that his temper was smoking as profusely as the volcano's crater—except Scout's eruption was imminent.

His work boots came to an abrupt halt directly in front of her, kicking sand up onto her knees. "Just what the hell is going on?"

Guilelessly, she smiled up at him from beneath the brim of her hat. "Hello, Scout. I'm so glad you joined us. Why don't you take a swim?"

"A sw-swim?" he stammered in disbelief. "I'm up there breaking my back for these people and they're down here playing on the beach, stringing flowers," he shouted, kicking a garland of plumeria aside, "taking the day off!

"I began to notice that the lunch break was sure stretching out, but being the nice taskmaster that I am, and considering this infernal heat, I thought, Hey, don't begrudge them a few extra minutes. But then the workers who did show up after lunch began disappearing one by one. Before I knew it, I was the only one doing any work."

"Then it was time you joined us, wasn't it? Sit down here in the shade and cool off before—"

"I don't want to sit down, Chantal. I don't want to cool off. We've almost got the bridge finished. All but a few steps have been cemented into place. We're about to see the end of this thing."

"Then taking one afternoon off won't hurt." Her poised reasonableness pushed him over the edge. He raised his balled fist to his temples and pounded them, cursing liberally. "You're only making yourself hotter," she said logically. "And you may as well relax, because the men aren't going back to work until tomorrow morning. Today has been declared a holiday."

"By whom? By you? Does your authority supersede mine?"

He had finally piqued her temper. She unfolded her legs and stood up. Her sandy, bare toes stood their ground against the heavy soles of his boots. A slender bikini was hardly a garb suitable for combat, but her eyes gleamed militantly.

"When it comes to the happiness and contentment of these people, yes, my authority supersedes yours. So does the authority of the village leaders. The high council complained to me that the workers were tired and in need of a day of rest. They aren't accustomed to working the long hours that you do."

"Well, I'm not exactly having fun over there, you know."

"Please lower your voice, Scout. You'll upset them."

"Upset *them*?" he repeated in a thin, irate voice. "I don't give a flying fig if I upset them." He jabbed his chest with his index finger. "In order for me to meet my deadline, I need every man on the job every hour of the workday. We've had enough delays, like looking for those chickens that got out of their pen the other day. It took hours to round them up, and everybody got in on the game. Then there was that episode about the generator having a bad spirit. Can you imagine how ridiculous I felt arguing a case for a generator? That kangaroo court took up half a day."

To make his final point, he inclined nearer, so that she had to lean back or be pressed against him. "They may not be accustomed to the long hours, but I'm not accustomed to workers walking off an unfinished job just because they damn well feel like it."

"This isn't the United States."

"No foolin'," he said drolly.

Determined to remain calm, Chantal spoke in a rigidly controlled tone. "They don't live according to deadlines. They aren't concerned with delays. They're islanders. Tomorrow will be exactly like today. Unlike the average American male, they aren't propelled by the drive to succeed. They work only for what they need.

"Personally, I believe that's an excellent policy to live by. And I'm sorry, Scout, but as long as you're on the island, you'll have to abide by that policy too."

He was gnawing the inside of his cheek, only one indication of his fury. His hair clung wetly to his forehead. Sweat had streaked his dirty face. His unbuttoned shirt was plastered to his torso. The pelt on his heaving chest was curly and wet with perspiration.

He looked delicious.

Because he was squinting against the afternoon sun, she couldn't see anything except slits beneath his brows. He was angry, she could tell, but she stared into the narrowed eyes resolutely, refusing to back down. The village men had been granted a well-earned day off. She wasn't going to renege on it and force them back to work. Scout would just have to understand. If understanding was beyond him, he would just have to tolerate it.

Suddenly he raised his arm. Chantal flinched, thinking he might strike her. All he did was consult the face of his wristwatch. "Okay, I'm reasonable," he said. "It's one o'clock now. They can wait out the hottest part of the day. But at four, playtime is over. I want everyone to report back to work then. We'll get in a few hours work before dark."

"You can't expect them to work this evening," she exclaimed.

"The hell I can't. I've got a job to do and I want to see it done."

"What's your hurry? Your fiancée?"

"For starters."

Her own eyes narrowed dangerously. He had provoked her into a shouting match. She, in turn, had goaded him. His comeback had hurt, but she couldn't allow it to distract her from the original argument. "They are not coming back to work today, period."

He bent back his hand, thrust his wrist so close to her face that it almost touched the tip of her nose, and tapped the crystal of his watch. "Four o'clock, Chantal. Not a second later."

She acted before she thought. Swifter than a human eye could follow, she slid the elastic watchband from his wrist and flung the thing into the seawater thrashing against the nearest boulder.

"You'll have difficulty measuring the seconds now, Mr. Ritland."

Scout gaped at the surging wave that was now being sucked back to sea. "That was a Rolex!"

"In this village it has less value than a garland of flowers and isn't nearly as pretty."

If he could have taken a step closer, he would

have. Since they were already standing toe to toe, he had to settle for angling his body against hers, finally making contact. Through clenched teeth he warned, "I'm gonna strangle you yet."

Chantal tossed back her head and arched her throat, offering it up to him defiantly, daring him to do what he had threatened. Accepting the challenge, he raised his hand to the base of her neck. His fingers encircled it. His thumb pressed against her warmly throbbing pulse.

For long moments they stared into each other's eyes. Then he lowered his gaze to focus on her mouth. Involuntarily responding, her lips parted in mute appeal.

A low groan originated deep in his chest and emerged as a curse. He wavered between pulling her to him or pushing her away, finally opting for pushing her. He went stamping down the beach, leaning heavily on Johnny, who had devotedly rushed to his side. Chantal, breathless and disturbed, watched him until he disappeared.

"Chantal?"

She realized that André had spoken her name several times, trying to get her attention. "I'm sorry. What is it?"

"Did he hurt you?"

"Oh, no, no," she hastily assured him. "He didn't understand why everyone was taking the day off. I had to explain it to him."

His eyes were full of suspicion and hostility as he glanced in the direction Scout had gone. "Never mind him, André," she said. "Enjoy the day."

He rejoined a group of young people, among them the lovely Margot. Chantal sank back onto the sand, finally giving way to the weakness in her knees, an aftereffect of her altercation with Scout. Leaning against the trunk of a palm, she closed her eyes and tried to regulate her heart rate and breathing.

It was becoming more and more difficult to resist him. In the evenings when she felt his penetrating stare on her, she wanted to respond the way her body urged her to. She wanted to go to him as a woman, please him, appease the hunger she knew was eating at him. She wanted to, but she couldn't.

Her pride wouldn't allow it. She wouldn't be used then discarded and left behind when he returned to Jennifer, who would be the perfect wife for him.

She had the islanders' loyalty and protection. If the need arose, she would be protected from Scout's appetite for her. What she feared most was her appetite for him. Her conscience offered little protection against that.

"How much farther?" Scout paused on the trail to mop his face with a handkerchief that was already saturated. "Miles?"

Johnny gazed up at him bemusedly.

"The heat must really be getting to me. I'm talking to a kid who doesn't understand a word I'm saying. But that makes about as much sense as anything that's happened to me since I followed the island princess out of the Coral Reef's ballroom. Should have known she was too good to be true, Johnny. Beware of women in white who look and move and talk like goddesses. Sooner or later there'll be hell to pay."

Johnny smiled dubiously.

Scout sighed and began hiking again. They'd left the village hours earlier. He had reasoned that if he couldn't get anywhere with Chantal, he might be able to talk some sense into her old man.

Scout predicted that the Frenchman would be crazier than a bedbug. Otherwise, why would he choose to stay in these overgrown foothills, where every insect known to man, and a few that were unknown, thrived? The heat was unbearable. He felt like a Thanksgiving turkey basting in his own sweat.

Always at his right was Voix de Tonnerre. Every once in a while it would discharge molten rock and steam as if to remind him that it was still an ever-present threat to be reckoned with. Could any human abide this climate?

Apparently, George duPont could. Scout was positive he had made Johnny understand whom he wanted to see. The boy had nodded eagerly and pointed toward the hills on the other side of the ravine when Scout asked him where duPont could be found.

"I know he's in the foothills," Scout had replied patiently, "but *where* in the foothills?" Through sign language Scout communicated that he wanted to be led to the old man. They'd left the village minutes later. Now Scout was beginning to question the wisdom of this impulsive trek. When they set out, he had had no idea how far they had to go. He was hot, thirsty, and his wounded leg had begun to ache.

As soon as they reached the summit of the far side of the ravine, he had discovered the jeep. It was covered with military camouflage netting. His heart had leapt with excitement. There were no keys in the ignition, but he probably could have hot-wired it.

One look at Johnny's mournful eyes and trembling lower lip, however, changed his mind. He couldn't lay the burden of his escape on the kid.

Besides, he wouldn't leave the bridge unfinished. The midwestern work ethic that had been drilled into him by his blue-collar father would never have allowed his conscience a moment's peace if he did.

Anyway, he was curious to meet George duPont, who was probably brilliant but eccentric. Corey Reynolds had trusted the Frenchman's expert opinion on Voix de Tonnerre. His company had invested millions to build the resort, so he must have thought the volcanologist knew his stuff.

There was another reason he'd resisted the temptation to take the jeep. Chantal. She trusted him to finish her bridge. He had told her he would. He couldn't just walk out on her. If he did, she would lose face with the people, who obviously adored her. And, well, he couldn't just up and leave without even saying good-bye.

"I'm too damn honorable for my own good," he had muttered to Johnny. "A freaking boy scout." Johnny had nodded in somber agreement and looked relieved when they left the jeep exactly as they had found it.

Now, hours of walking and liters of sweat later, Johnny suddenly plunged ahead through the jungle, chattering in French and pointing vigorously toward the top of a steep incline.

"Up there?" Scout asked dejectedly.

"*Oui.*"

"Great." Scout released a heavy sigh and began climbing the winding, rocky path. At one point he stopped to rest. Cupping his hands around his mouth, he called out loudly, "George duPont?"

Jungle birds screeched their objections to having their peace disturbed. "Mr. duPont, my name is Scout Ritland. I'd like to see you, sir. I'm sure your daughter has told you about me."

He waited. No response. The old man could be hard of hearing. He assumed duPont spoke English, but it occurred to him that he didn't know that for certain. Why waste his breath until he confronted the scientist face-to-face?

Favoring his hurt leg, he labored up the hill. Johnny assisted him up the last few grueling yards. When he reached the plateau, he bent at the waist and placed his hands on his knees as he waited to regain his breath.

Sweat poured down his face and dripped off the tip of his nose, ran into the collar of his sodden shirt, and collected in his eyebrows. Some trickled into his eyes, making them sting. As he gradually straightened, he wiped them with the backs of his hands, but since they were sweat-slippery, too, that did little good.

His eyes were cloudy and stinging. That was why he didn't at first believe the sight he beheld. He blinked several times and shook his head in bafflement.

There were two of them on top of the hill overlooking the South Pacific vista. Each was covered with a blanket of flowers and marked with a small white cross.

Graves.

Chantal patted the child on the head and told him not to get the injury wet for several days. He'd fallen over a sharp rock while playing on the beach and scraped his shin. She had been summoned to treat the deep scratch, then was pressed to share the family's evening meal. It was a show of their appreciation, an invitation she couldn't decline.

All during the meal, however, her thoughts had been on Scout and his whereabouts. She hadn't seen either him or Johnny since they'd left the beach together. When she had returned to the house, she had expected to find him there, sulking. She wouldn't have been surprised to find him stubbornly working on the bridge, even though his crew had deserted him. But he'd been in neither place.

As the afternoon stretched into evening, she became more apprehensive. At sunset she had sent for André.

"Go check on the jeep."

"Why?"

She had been tempted to snap "Just do it," but had curbed her impatience. "I can't locate Mr. Ritland. Have you seen him?"

At that moment she had felt a stab of fear that maybe André was responsible for Scout's disappearance. However, as soon as that thought crossed her mind, she dismissed it. She had been listening to Scout too long. He was turning her suspicious of friends she had known and trusted all her life.

While André was on the errand, she paced. When he returned and reported that the jeep was where he'd left it, she didn't know whether to be relieved or concerned.

"Take a few men and look around. See if you can find him."

"After I do?"

"Bring him back."

Without any further discussion, André had left to do as she asked. He hadn't returned yet. The longer he was gone, the more worried she became.

Now, as she bade the injured boy and his family good night and wended her way through the village carrying her father's first aid bag, she wondered again where he could be.

Darkness had fallen. The rugged terrain could be dangerous even to people who had lived on the island all their lives. Scout didn't know where to look for danger. He abused his wounded left leg, which wasn't as strong as he wanted to believe it was.

What if he had fallen on it? What if he were lying somewhere helpless and bleeding? What if Johnny were afraid to return to the village and report that the person he had been commissioned to watch had eluded him in the darkness?

Frowning with anxiety, she entered her house and replaced the medical bag on the shelf, where it could always be located in an emergency. The house was dark. No lamps had been lit during her absence. Scout had not returned.

But then she caught a whiff of a faint and familiar scent.

Her heart leapt within her chest and began to flutter. Timorously, she followed the scent toward the kitchen. Telling herself her fears were silly and that there were no such things as cigar-smoking ghosts, she nevertheless hesitated a moment before pushing open the bamboo door.

The red tip of the lighted cigar winked at her through the darkness. She gasped.

"What are you doing?"

"Taking a bath."

Scout was lounging in the portable copper tub, his knees poking out of the surface of the water. His hair was wet and appeared to have been shampooed and rinsed, then pushed back off his forehead with his fingers.

"I mean with—"

"The cigar?" he asked nonchalantly. He took a deep puff and sent several smoke rings floating ceilingward. "I don't think George would mind if I borrowed one, do you?"

Swallowing with difficulty, Chantal shook her head no.

"You little liar."

Scout placed the burning cigar in a ceramic ashtray which he'd put on the seat of the chair nearest him. He rested his arms on the rim of the tub, letting his hands dangle over the water. His fingers flicked it, sending up little splashes that she could hear better than she could see. For something so innocent, they sounded quite ominous, almost as sinister as his sibilant voice.

"I had quite an afternoon," he said. "Very informative. I guess I should thank you for insisting that I take the day off. I got to see a part of the island I'd never seen."

He picked up the cigar and puffed again. "Of course, I sweated off about ten pounds, overworked my left leg until it started hurting like a sonofabitch, got attacked by a swarm of man-eating insects, came face-to-face with a snake as big around as my waist, and barely survived a rock slide. Other than that, it was a terrific day in paradise. And it was worth all those hardships to get to meet your father."

His whispery voice had gradually risen until the last sentence was a bona fide shout. Chantal shuddered with dread. Closing her eyes, she tried to regain her balance and decide how she was going to placate a man who obviously had homicide in mind.

"I'll explain everything. As soon as you've finished your bath, I'll see you in the living room."

"You'll see me now."

He stood up suddenly, creating a tidal wave in the tub that sloshed onto the floor. Slinging water and swear words in equal proportions, he stepped out of the tub and bore down on her. Chantal uttered a squeak of fear and spun around to retreat.

She wasn't fast enough. Scout's fist enclosed a handful of fabric and jerked her to a staggering halt. His biceps bunched as he curled his arm and brought her around to face him. He pressed his fist against her spine, flattening her against his chest. His head came down until the bath water on his face dripped onto hers.

"Why didn't you tell me he was dead?"

"I didn't think it would be wise."

"Because you'd hold more sway over me if I thought your old man was still around, right?"

"Right. I didn't think you would trust my opinions about anything as much as you would trust his."

"Trust is a funny word for you to be tossing around, princess," he said scornfully, pressing her harder against him. "When did he die?"

"About a week before I kidnapped you." Chantal saw that her answer surprised him. He hadn't realized that George's death had been so recent. She liked him for letting a moment of respectful silence lapse before barraging her with more questions.

"What happened?"

"He just . . ." She paused to clear the emotional knot from her throat and to blink tears from her eyes. "He was coming back from a trip up to the volcano and just . . . died. Heart attack, I suppose."

"You didn't notify anybody?"

"No."

"You didn't want anybody to know he was dead?"

"No."

"Why not?"

"It didn't matter to anybody except me and the villagers."

"And they couldn't tell me because none of them, except André, can speak English."

"That's right," she conceded softly. "Father wanted to be buried next to my mother. Eventually, his death certificate will have to be filed with the authorities, but what difference will it make what date is on it?"

She could feel his hard stare on her uplifted face. She returned it unflinchingly. Her actions had been unorthodox but, to her mind, necessary. She wasn't going to start stammering explanations or excuses for them now.

Finally, he said, "I gotta hand it to you—you're clever."

"Not clever. Desperate."

"Who devised the scheme to get me here, you or your father? Whose idea was it to use you as a lure?"

She lowered her eyes then and addressed his chin. "Mine."

"And the gun?"

"Father was against using violence of any kind. He thought you could probably be reasoned with and convinced to help us. André and I had our doubts."

"So when the old man died, you went with your plan."

"Yes. I asked André to get the gun." Her chin went up a notch. "And we were right to do it that way. You couldn't have been persuaded to help us if we hadn't used force."

"Okay, so you got me here and I agreed to help you out of your jam. Why have you kept your father's death a secret all this time? What purpose did it serve?"

Her defiance faltered again. "If you believed that he was still around, if you thought that he might return at any time unannounced, then . . . then . . ."

The light of understanding dawned in his eyes. "Then you'd be safe from me."

"It's worked," she declared.

"Up till now, princess."

His lips seized hers savagely. With one arm across her shoulders and the other curved around her narrow waist, he lifted her off her feet and against his nakedness.

Chantal was stunned when her bare thighs collided with warm skin, soft hair, and hard masculinity. Another rocket of surprising sensation went through her when he thrust his tongue between her lips.

His mouth tasted clean, as though he had recently brushed his teeth. He smelled of soap and cigars and aroused maleness. The hunger for him, which had been smoldering like the heart of the volcano, spontaneously consumed her. She responded as she wanted to, not as her conscience dictated. Her starved body gave her no choice.

She pressed her tongue against his. Scout registered surprise. He pulled back. Waited. Then, around a yearning sound, melded his mouth with hers again.

She clasped him around the waist and ran her hands over the smooth, muscular expanse of his back. Drops of water still clung to his skin, wetting her fingertips as they kneaded the supple flesh of his buttocks.

Fervently, wildly, he began kissing her neck, his beard stubble lightly scraping her skin. She arched her neck back so far, her hair almost touched the backs of her knees. It whisked against his bare thighs.

He raised his head and gazed down at her. The front of her shirt was wet. The cloth had been molded to her breasts. He laid his hands on her collarbone, then slowly combed them down over her chest.

His fingers skimmed over her breasts, drawing the tips into prominent peaks. He kissed one through the wet cloth, flicking his tongue across it again and again, then taking a gentle love bite from the soft mound surrounding it. Reflexively, her body bowed, tilting her hips against his and making electrifying contact.

"Ah, dear Lord." He cupped her derriere to hold her still and tight against him. Burying his face in the hollow of her shoulder, he whispered roughly, "I want you. Sleep with me, Chantal. Please."

Perhaps if he hadn't said anything . . . Perhaps if he hadn't reminded her that any relationship between them would be temporary and strictly physical . . . Perhaps . . .

Instead, she became tense and unreceptive when he took her face between his hands and kissed her mouth with slow deliberation. Sensing her nonparticipation, he lifted his head and looked at her inquiringly.

"I can't," she cried softly, her voice tearing with emotion. "I'm sorry. I can't."

Before he could detain and persuade her, either of which he could easily do, she bolted past him and ran through the back door.

He rushed after her, but was brought up short when dark shadows separated themselves from the shrubbery. The needle-sharp tip of a spear came up against his navel.

"What the hell!"

Chantal stopped her headlong rush down to the beach. She spun around, then sucked in a sharp breath of alarm.

"Oh, no!"

André and several other young men of the village had Scout surrounded. All were armed with knives and spears. Their faces were intent, their stances dangerous.

"Call off your watchdogs, Chantal," he said in a steely rasp.

She addressed the menacing circle of men. One by one they backed away from him and sheathed their weapons. André was the last to withdraw. He did so with visible reluctance. "We tracked him here," he reported to Chantal.

"You sent them after me?" Moments ago Scout's face had been flushed with passion. Now it was white with rage.

"I didn't know where you were," she said defensively. "I thought you might be in danger."

"Like hell you did," he snarled. "You thought I might escape before your damn bridge was finished. Which, if I had exercised common sense, I would have done." He pointed his finger at her. "I wouldn't touch you now if you were the last woman on this island and I was stuck here for eternity. Fortunately, neither is the case."

With that, he knocked aside the young man standing in his path and stalked into the house, letting the door slam shut behind him.

Eleven

An eruption from Voix de Tonnerre woke Chantal the following morning. The atmosphere was still, hot, and humid. Explosive. She wondered uneasily if that portended how the rest of the day would go.

Leaving her bed, she washed and dressed. She was alone in the house. Scout wasn't in the kitchen, where he could usually be found at this time of day, drinking cup after cup of strong black coffee. When she had returned from her swim the night before, he had been gone. Apparently, he hadn't returned all night. In the mood he was in, she wasn't surprised.

She breakfasted on fruit and coffee, then went outside. The sun was just rising above the mountain peaks, but she heard the ring of a pickax against metal. Even this early, the village was unnaturally quiet as she walked through it on her way to the work site. Standing on the cliff looking down, she saw Scout far below. His olive drab tank top already showed a dark strip of perspiration down the center of his chest.

She had taken enough psychology courses in college to recognize him as a type A personality, an overachiever, one driven to do everything well. He pushed himself to the limit, as he was doing now. Before any of the villagers reported for work, he was already hard at it, taking on the responsibility himself. No wonder the slow pace of life on the island irritated him.

He paused to mop his face with a handkerchief. As he did, he spotted her. His expression was antagonistic. She winced as though in pain because his blatant animosity hurt her. Not that she could blame him for it after the events of last night. Such unmitigated rejection would be an insult to any man's ego.

It was her prerogative to say no, of course. Still, she hadn't liked doing so. She would much rather Scout be looking at her with drowsy desire, as he had before, as he—

"Mademoiselle?"

When the word was spoken, Chantal started with guilty surprise and turned. Members of the village's governing council had collected around her. Their demeanor was serious. Few would meet her eyes directly.

"What is it?" She sensed that they had come to impart something of utmost gravity, but she underestimated the severity of it. When they stated their business, it affected her like a physical blow. "Are you sure?"

To a man, they grimly nodded.

"Say, what's going on?" Scout took the last few steps that had been cemented into the steep walls of the ravine only days before. Having made the climb, he was short of breath. "Where is everybody?"

Chantal gazed at him, her eyes searching his, wanting to see honesty and integrity and an unbreachable code of morality there. "They won't be coming to work today."

"What? Don't tell me they're taking another day off?"

"They won't be coming to work today, or tomorrow, or ever."

He shifted weight off his left leg. For several seconds he stared at her, then he gave the group of elderly men a puzzled glance. "Somebody want to fill me in on what the hell's going on? We could have this thing finished with a few days hard work from everybody. What's the matter with you people?"

Chantal was the only one who understood him. It fell to her to explain the problem. "You, Mr. Ritland. You are what is the matter."

"Me?" he exclaimed, flattening a hand over his sweaty chest. "I've bent over backward to accommodate them and their customs. I gave them the day off yesterday. I—"

"You seduced one of the village girls and stole her virginity."

The words fell like stones around them. Scout's jaw hung slack while he gaped at Chantal with patent disbelief. Then he fashioned a smile. "This is a joke, right?"

"Do they look like they're joking?" Perilously close to tears, she angrily flung her hand in the direction of the village's high council. "They don't consider a manipulative and selfish seduction a laughing matter, Mr. Ritland."

"And I don't consider a false accusation one either," he fired back.

"Then you're denying it?"

"Damn right! When was this seduction supposed to have taken place?"

"Last night." Chantal's chest felt tight and constricted. She barely had sufficient air to speak, but she forced the words out. With vicious clarity she remembered his angry departure speech of the night before. "I refused to sleep with you, so you sought out Margot and seduced her. Feel better now? Did your lusts get satisfied?"

"Whatever lusts I had, you incited, princess."

An involuntary sob escaped her trembling lips. "I offered myself to you in exchange for building the bridge. Couldn't you simply have reminded me of that and left Margot alone?"

Scout's hands balled into fists at his sides. "She's only a kid, for chrissake."

"She was until last night."

"I haven't even been alone with her."

"You think she's pretty."

"She is! I'd have to be blind not to notice. But that's a long way from forcing myself on her."

"She says otherwise."

"Then she's lying."

"She wouldn't."

"Well, neither would I! The only noted liar around here is *you*!"

The betrayal she felt was so painful, the insult went almost unnoticed. She wanted to hear his vehement denial of the charge, but only if it was the truth. Why would Margot lie? She put that question to Scout.

"I don't know, but she is."

"Last night you said—"

"Forget what I said." He made a slicing, dismissive gesture. "I was mad, granted. I spouted off and said things I probably shouldn't have, but I spent the night on the beach. Alone. Believe me, Chantal."

"It doesn't matter what I believe. Their opinion is the one that counts."

"Not to me."

She stared into his face for several long moments, wanting desperately to believe him. His eyes were steady, reflecting not a glimmer of mendacity. Her gut instincts regarding people were seldom wrong. He had his faults, but she didn't believe that seducing teenage girls was one of them.

Finally, she turned and addressed the council, telling them that Scout denied Margot's allegations. They muttered among themselves, periodically casting him suspicious glances.

"What are they saying?"

"That's Margot's father." She pointed out the man who was making the most strenuous arguments. "He's saying that he and her mother caught Margot crying this morning. When they urged her to tell them what was wrong, she said she was ashamed for giving up her virginity to the American, to you. They're trying to decide what would be a befitting test of your honesty."

"Test? What kind of test? I—"

She held up her hand to stave off his protests and listened while the decision was handed down by the councilman who had been appointed spokesperson. Chantal heard him out, then inclined her head as though agreeing with their ruling.

"Well?" Scout demanded. "Are they talking about shrinking my head, or what?"

She faced him, drawing herself up to her full height. "No, they're talking about sending you to the volcano."

"This is *nuts!*" Scout slapped aside an enormous frond merely because it had had the misfortune to be in the wrong place at the wrong time—in his path. "I can't believe my fate is being dictated by a bunch of witch doctors in loincloths."

He swatted at an insect that buzzed close to his face. "When I get back to the States, I'm going to sell my story to a Hollywood producer. Come to think of it, though, no one would buy it because it's too implausible."

"Your mouthing is only making you more short-winded. Why not save your breath?"

He spun around to confront Chantal on the overgrown path leading up the hillside. "You know this is a bunch of crap, don't you? A waste of time and energy. Why'd you let them talk you into it?"

"For the same reason I've done everything else: The bridge. You can't finish it alone. The people won't work for you until you've proved yourself worthy and have been blessed by Voix de Tonnerre."

He muttered his low opinion of the mission. He had originally been revered and respected as one sent by the gods. Margot's accusation had placed his divinity in doubt. The council had decided that he must travel to Voix de Tonnerre and leave an offering. If he accomplished that without being harmed, they would again believe in him. It would be a sign that his presence in the village had been divinely inspired.

He glared down at her. "For all I know, you cooked up those charges against me so you could go to the volcano and take your damn close-ups." He indicated the heavy camera bag she was carrying on her shoulder.

"Somebody had to come along to verify that you didn't leave the offering just any old place. It so happens that besides my father, I'm the one most familiar with the volcano." She hoisted the camera bag to a more comfortable position on her shoulder. "You're wasting not only your breath, but my time, Mr. Ritland. Proceed, please."

Swearing beneath his breath, he did.

They walked for hours through the dense jungle in the foothills before they began to climb the mountain nearest the crater of Voix de Tonnerre. The weight of the camera and its gear began to make the muscles of Chantal's neck, shoulders, and back ache to the point of burning.

Scout carried their provisions along with a knapsack filled with a token offering from each villager. The load began to take its toll on him. Unconsciously, he favored his left leg. They stopped frequently to drink from their water canteens, but they sweated out the fluid almost as soon as it was swallowed.

Eventually, they left the jungle behind. The ground became rockier and steeper, with little vegetation. There was more of a breeze, but the air became gradually thinner and warmer.

When it seemed there was no relief in sight, they came to a sheer cliff rising out of a plateau. A waterfall cascaded down the cliff into a pool. Chantal dropped her camera gear, removed her boots, and dove headfirst into the water. Scout did likewise. They emerged dripping wet.

Chantal sat down on the boulder and took a long drink from her canteen. She wrung the water out of her long braid and replaced the straw hat on her head to shade her face. She caught Scout watching her closely.

"Your father's?"

"What?" Then, realizing that he was referring to the straw hat, she nodded. "Yes. I knew I could never fill his shoes," she said with a wistful smile, "so I thought I'd try his hat."

"I figured something like that. And all that scribbling you do every night?"

"The last chapter of the textbook he was working on."

"You're finishing it for him."

She saw no reason to lie. "That's why I wanted to be unspecific about the date of his death. The publishers don't need to know that he didn't compile and record all the data himself."

"You won't get any credit for it."

"I don't want any," she replied, surprised that he would even think that she might. "For all the courses

I took, even in graduate school, my father was the best teacher I ever had. The soul of the volcano was inside him. He felt it like a heartbeat in his chest. He knew it intimately. The only thing I can take credit for is being his most devoted pupil."

Scout continued to look at her, his gaze intent. "I've never laid a hand on that girl, Chantal. Surely you don't believe I did."

Her brow puckered doubtfully. "In your condition—"

"In my condition, I could have bedded a hundred women, but it wouldn't have done any good. There's only one woman I want. You."

Her belly quickened; she took a sudden little breath. She wanted to denounce this burst of elation, but it was too strong. She had been disillusioned to think he could compromise a young girl, but jealousy was at the root of her reaction to the alleged crime. She couldn't bear the thought of him desiring another woman. It drove her mad to imagine him making love to someone else. This ungenerous but very human attitude shocked her. Just how deeply did her feelings for Scout run?

She was uneasy with the answer that formed in her mind and for the time being refused to acknowledge it.

"We'd better go." She laced her boots and prepared to leave. When she hoisted the camera case to her shoulder, Scout took it from her.

"Let me carry that."

"It's too heavy."

"That's why I need to carry it." He equalized his loads, dividing the weight of them between his shoulders. "There. Now I'm balanced. How much farther?"

"A mile, maybe more. It's rugged terrain from here on."

"More rugged than it's been?"

"I'm afraid so. Almost straight up."

"Lead on," he said tiredly. "I'm right behind you."

There was no path. They stumbled over rocky ground to reach the peak of the mountain nearest Voix de Tonnerre, which provided them an excellent vantage point. It was hot; the very air they breathed scorched their lungs. Yet, it was an exhilarating climb.

Chantal's pulse began to pound with more than physical exertion. It raced with excitement, which it never failed to do when she came this close to the volcano. Glancing over her shoulder at Scout, she saw that he shared her feelings. He was staring with awe and wonder at this powerful force of nature which seemed to have a distinct personality.

From its mouth it spewed fire. The lava runs were red rivulets that crawled down the slopes of the cone. The air thundered with each fiery belch. The ground vibrated beneath them.

"Goda'mighty," Scout said in awe, "it's magnificent, isn't it?"

"I love it."

"Just think, the material it's spitting out will be here millions of years from now. We're witnessing a birth."

Chantal, gratified by Scout's insight, stood on a cliff, silhouetted against the red sky. The hot wind molded her clothes to her body. She removed her father's hat and unwound her braid, allowing her hair to whip wildly around her. The glow in the atmosphere made her skin look like polished bronze. She could have been a high priestess paying homage to her pagan deity.

Scout moved up beside her. "Thank you for sharing this with me."

Her gaze swung around to his. They remained locked in each other's stare until the earth trembled with a vigorous eruption. Rocks were shaken loose and went tumbling over the cliff beneath them.

Chantal smiled when Scout's face registered some anxiety. "If you're innocent of seducing Margot, you've nothing to fear from Voix de Tonnerre."

"I'm innocent, but I'll feel a whole lot better once we leave this sack of junk, take our pictures, and get the hell out of here."

Because each was growing anxious, they resorted to humor to alleviate their fear. "I don't think your attitude is properly penitent, Mr. Ritland," she chided teasingly.

"I'm new to this, you know. What am I supposed to do, spit into my palms and turn around three times while chanting something about being a good boy from now on?"

"You're making fun of us, of our culture."

"*Their* culture. You don't believe in this hocus-pocus any more than I do. You're only pretending you do to annoy me." He emptied the sack of offerings and began scattering them around. "While I'm doing this, get busy on those pictures, will you? I think highly of Voix de Tonnerre, but I'm not sure how he feels about us."

She set up a tripod and attached her camera. Methodically, she began snapping pictures, each more fantastic than the one before. She went through one roll of film, then another. The sun set and the sky grew dark, although it was hard to tell because Voix de Tonnerre bathed everything with a rich rosy glow.

"Time to go, don't you think?" Scout asked warily.

"Yes. I hate to. It will be years before it has another eruption of this magnitude." Her voice was sad. Scout efficiently repacked her camera gear while she watched the exploding mountaintop with a mix of reverence and regret.

He touched her elbow, then laid his hand along her cheek and brushed away a tear with his thumb. "Chantal? Princess? I know you hate to leave. I hate to make you. But we've got to get down this slope before it gets any darker."

"*Au revoir*," she whispered. Then she turned and placed her hand in the one Scout extended to her.

Because he now carried a lighter load and gravity was working for them, they made faster progress going down than they had on the climb up. Chantal knew his leg must be aching, but his jaw was set against the pain. He seemed to care more for her safety than for his own. Several times she lost her footing and would have slid down the steep incline if he hadn't blocked her fall with his own body.

"The volcano does realize that those offerings were from us, doesn't it?" he asked, glancing over his shoulder worriedly as Voix de Tonnerre shot a geyser of fire and molten rock into the night sky. The eruptions were coming quickly on the heels of each other, with decreasing time in between.

"I'm not afraid. Are you?"

"Hell no," he staunchly declared.

Then both laughed and scrambled more hastily down the mountainside, giving up any pretense of not running for their lives. The volcanic eruptions were increasingly violent. Ash and cinder fell around them like incendiary snow.

"Quick, into the water!" Scout shouted at her when they reached the pool where they had found relief before.

"Wait. This is fabulous." She whipped the camera out of the bag on his shoulder and began clicking off pictures as quickly as the motor drive would allow. "Oh, look at that!"

"Chantal."

"If only Father could see—"

"*Chantal!*"

He yanked the camera from her, tossed it onto the ground, and did a cannonball into the pool, taking her with him. The water closed over their heads. Scout found the bottom first and jackknifed his knees to shoot them to the surface. When their heads cleared it, Voix de Tonnerre was exploding.

Nothing to that point equaled this furious expulsion. Fire rained from the sky. Cinders striking the water around them sizzled and died. They could do nothing but gape, awe superseding their fear.

Scout had likened it to a birth. It was as thrilling, as painful, as beautiful. It seemed to go on forever.

And then it stopped.

The sudden quiet was deafening.

For long minutes they remained standing chin-high in the water. Finally, Scout took her hand and waded out of the pool. Only puffs of harmless white smoke were being emitted from the volcano now. It looked benevolent.

Chantal dropped to her knees in exhaustion. Scout lowered himself beside her. It seemed inappropriate to speak, so neither said anything. Eventually, Scout lay down and drew her close. He curled his body protectively around hers.

Overhead, clouds of ash were swept out to sea by a cooling breeze.

Twelve

Chantal woke up and disengaged herself from Scout's arms. Or, rather, she tried. He clasped her arms as she sat up. His eyes came open. Holding her, he gazed up into her face. He touched her hair, her cheek.

His expression was inquisitive and eloquent. Was he asking her if it had felt good to sleep beside him all night? Could he read in her returned stare that it had?

She wanted to bend down and plant a soft, sweet, good-morning kiss on his lips. If she did, however, she wouldn't want to stop with that and knew that she must. If she lay down with Scout a second longer, she would never want to leave his side.

Calling upon reserves of self-discipline that would have done a monk proud, she eased her arms from his grasp and stood up. She examined her camera and discovered that it had suffered no serious damage the night before. The rolls of film she had taken were all intact and still encased in their canisters.

It took Scout longer to get up and stirring about. His joints were stiff from having slept in wet clothing. Obviously, his wounded left leg was sore again. She caught him unconsciously rubbing it when he bent down to refill their canteens with water from the pool.

"You don't have your hat," he observed as they left the area.

"I lost it last night when we were running down the mountain."

"You should have said something. I'm sorry."

"I'm not. Father would like to know it's somewhere at the foot of Voix de Tonnerre."

They had little to say, but, oddly, were communicating better than they ever had. They were also distinctly aware of each other. Countless times they stopped simultaneously and just stared into each other's eyes, as though their encompassing interest had rendered them immobile.

They had shared something unique, and it seemed to have forged a bond that linked them together in an irreversible way. Or maybe this new sense of closeness stemmed from having passed the night wrapped in the other's warmth.

Something significant had happened. It went beyond the sexual and bordered on the spiritual. They felt the change; they just couldn't define it. And for the present, each seemed content to savor it without labeling it.

Their arrival at the village was heralded. Drums began to beat long before they reached the ravine. As soon as they stepped through the foliage, a cheer went up from the throng gathered on the other side.

Chantal smiled up at Scout. "It seems you're the hero of the day."

They carefully worked their way down the new steps on one side of the ravine, crossing the incomplete bridge with caution, then climbing up the other side. By the time they got halfway up, they were met by those who couldn't wait to pay homage to Scout.

"What are they saying?" he asked. Johnny had fought the other children for possession of Scout's hand. He was awarded the privilege of walking beside the hero and did so with enormous pride.

"The eruption last night was a sign of Voix de Tonnerre's favor. They're convinced that their confidence in you was not misplaced."

"Thank God. I'd hate to have to dynamite those steps out." He was grinning foolishly, enjoying the acclaim. He graciously accepted bouquets and leis and the other tokens of appreciation that were pressed on him.

But suddenly a hush fell over the jubilant crowd. It neatly parted as a small figure wended her way through. Chantal and Scout watched curiously until Margot stood before them with her head bowed so low they couldn't see her face for a curtain of hair.

In a barely audible whisper she spoke. When she was finished with her heart-wrenching speech, Chantal looked up at Scout. "Well?"

"She says that she lied about you." Chantal cleared her throat of emotional huskiness. "It seems her lover told her to accuse you of what he had done. She was afraid. She loves this man and wanted to do what he asked her to. But she couldn't live with her lie. Last night, afraid of the volcano's wrath, she told her parents the truth."

Scout looked down at the contrite girl. His eyes were filled with compassion, not censure. "Tell her I accept her apology and am willing to let the whole matter drop."

"It's not that simple, Scout."

"Why not?"

"They must be punished."

He looked alarmed. "What'll happen to her?"

"The council decided that her punishment is the shame she must bear."

"What about the guy?"

"It's up to you to exact his punishment, since he was the instigator of the crime against you."

"Who is it?"

Chantal put the question to Margot. Tears filled the girl's liquid eyes. Through trembling lips, she mumbled, "André."

No sooner had the name been spoken than there was another disturbance at the edge of the crowd. It worked its way toward them until André was shoved forward to stand before the man he had falsely accused.

To his credit, he stood proudly, his chin at a belligerent angle. His hands were tied in front of him, but he looked at Scout with open defiance.

"What are you going to do to him?"

Scout was swapping hostile stares with André, but when Chantal asked him the question, he looked down at her with apprehension.

She repeated the question. "You were the victim of his deceit. It's up to you to decide upon and inflict his punishment."

Scout raked his fingers through his hair. "If I'd wanted to be a judge, I'd have gone to law school. Can't we just shake hands and forget this mess?"

"No," she said adamantly, shaking her head. "They expect you to punish him. He expects to be punished. It will be worse for him if you don't. He would rather you kill him than lose face."

André remained silent, but his eyes echoed Chantal's words. "All right," Scout said grimly. "Somebody give me a knife."

Chantal gave a startled reaction, but the requested

knife was passed from hand to hand until it reached hers. She laid it in the palm of his hand.

"Remember, you got me into this," he said in an undertone, then turned to confront his adversary. He pressed the tip of the knife against André's belly as André had done to him two nights before.

"Your punishment for taking Margot's virginity is to marry her and give her many children."

André hadn't flinched when Scout pressed the knife against his abdomen, but he did then. He blinked and looked uncertainly toward Chantal, as though he wasn't sure he had heard correctly.

The villagers urged her to translate for them. When she did, they reacted audibly. Margot's head snapped up. She abruptly ceased praying; her rosary dangled from hands that had fallen still.

"Ask her if she loves him," Scout directed Chantal. She posed the question to Margot.

Her tears collected like dewdrops on her cheeks while she listened with breathless expectation. *"Oui, oui,"* she replied sincerely, bobbing her head. She babbled something more.

Chantal translated for Scout. "She says that if she hadn't loved him, she wouldn't have slept with him. But loving him as she does, expressing it was worth any price. Even shame. Even death."

Scout's attention snagged on Chantal's misty blue eyes for several seconds before he turned back to André. "You heard her. She loves you. Marry her. Give her children." He stepped closer to the man, nudging his belly with the tip of the knife, coming just short of breaking the skin. "If you ever mistreat her or even make her unhappy, I'll come back and make you a very unhappy eunuch." Easing back only slightly, he asked, "Do you accept this punishment?"

André, looking shaken, nodded.

"Good." With a quick motion that brought a collective gasp from the crowd, Scout slashed through the rope binding André's wrists. Then he flipped the knife, catching it by the tip of the blade, and extended the bone handle to André, who, in his confusion, took it. "Now that that's over, let's get back to work and finish this damn bridge."

"You've got them in the palm of your hand. Handing the knife to André and then turning your back to him won them over completely. Before that they admired you. Now they worship you."

Chantal and Scout were sitting together on a woven grass mat that just as well could have been a throne. The celebration to commemorate the completion of the bridge had begun at dusk. Since then, villagers had been presenting Scout with gifts.

Even as Chantal spoke, a giggling young girl placed a lei around his neck, kissed both his cheeks, then bolted for safety among her friends, from whom she had taken the dare.

"Lucky shot," he said laconically in response to Chantal's accurate observation. "The *punishment* I handed down seems to have worked." He nodded in the direction of the newlyweds, who were nuzzling affectionately while Margot's parents looked on with approval. "I guess André finally came to grips with the fact that he couldn't have you and took the next best thing."

Chantal avoided that touchy subject. "Margot will be a devoted wife. He's already teaching her English, which indicates to me that he not only loves her very much, but considers her his equal." She glanced over at Scout. "King Solomon couldn't have made a wiser judgment."

"You know about King Solomon?"

She sniffed her disapproval of his teasing. "I am not a heathen."

"Sometimes I wonder." His voice turned soft and low. "I remember how you looked standing against that exploding sky. I was scared spitless, but you gloried in the volcano's fury."

"It was glorious," she said simply. Then, to switch the conversation back to him, she added, "The men of the village respect your bravery. The women swoon over your handsomeness. They're all in love with you."

"*All?*"

For their entertainment, a ceremonial dance was being performed by a group of virile young men. Knives clacked, steel against steel. Spears were twirled like harmless batons. One dancer was juggling burning torches, slinging them end over end high into the air, then catching them before they reached the ground.

The dancers' agility and talent went largely unnoticed. Chantal and Scout had eyes only for each other. Since their return from the volcano, the pull between them had been as strong as the tide, and as incessant.

She loved him and was finally able to admit it to herself.

She loved his dedication to finishing the bridge. He worked hard and diligently, never content with results being merely satisfactory. Everything had to be done to perfection. He was a stern taskmaster, but asked nothing of his workers that he wasn't willing to do himself. He treated each man fairly. He didn't criticize mistakes or laziness, but complimented initiative and jobs done exceptionally well. He was a man of honor and compassion, as demonstrated by the way he had handled the problem with André and Margot.

She loved him passionately.

But he would leave her, and she didn't know how she would bear that.

"You'd better drink some more." She felt compelled to break the spell that had kept them staring at each other for a noticeably long time. "If you don't enjoy the party, their feelings will be hurt."

"If I drink much more, I won't have any feelings. My extremities are almost numb now." Nevertheless, he raised the coconut shell to his lips and drank deeply of the liquor, which he knew by now wasn't as innocent as it tasted.

"*Monsieur?*" An entire family approached and set a basket of fruit in front of him.

"*Merci.*"

Chantal was laughing at Scout's evident embarrassment as the man and his wife and children withdrew. "It still disconcerts you to speak to a bare-breasted woman."

"Too much of a Yankee Doodle Dandy, I guess."

"Where did you get your name?" She selected a ripe papaya from the basket and began to peel it.

"Scout?" He grinned boyishly. "When I was a kid, we used to play wagon train. I didn't want to be one of the pioneers going west to farm, see? I wanted to be the tough guy with a murky past. So I always wanted to play the scout. Kids in the neighborhood started calling me that, and it caught on." He shrugged. "Besides, it's a lot better than Winston Randolph, which is my real name."

"No!" she exclaimed as she bit into a succulent piece of the fruit.

"Yeah. Hell of a name for two people to stick on an innocent little baby, isn't it?"

"What is your family like?" she asked as she continued to peel the papaya.

"I'm all that's left. Both my parents are deceased."

"Oh."

"You're getting that stuff all over you."

He reached up to wipe away the dribbling papaya juice from her chin, then sucked it off his fingers. There was still juice on her lips. He studied it for several seconds, then leaned forward and licked it off, lightly skimming her lips with his tongue. Her lips parted, but she pulled back.

He groaned her name on a long, yearning sigh. His eyes roamed over her face, touching on each feature. "You're so incredibly beautiful."

"You're missing the dance. And they're performing in your honor." She could barely make herself heard above the drums and handmade flutes.

"I don't need to see it. I can feel the beat. In my head. In my heart. In my—" He swallowed hard and squeezed his eyes shut. "I've wanted you so damn bad. You don't know what agony it's been for me night after night to lie there under the same roof with you and not feel you against me as you were up there on the mountain."

"Scout—"

"Don't stop me. Hear me out. Something significant happened that night we slept together under Voix de Tonnerre." He spread his hands wide in a helpless gesture. "I don't know what it was exactly, but up to that night I thought maybe I was being seduced by this Bali H'ai and that you were just a part of it. But it's not like that, Chantal. It's you. I swear it's—"

The music ended abruptly. Everyone fell still. The dance was over. Scout's attention was momentarily diverted away from Chantal. He saw that the center of the ceremonial circle had been cleared. On the far side of it there was furtive movement, but nothing was happening yet.

When he turned to make a comment to Chantal, she was no longer sitting beside him. Impossible. He hadn't felt her move. He hadn't even felt the air stir. He swiveled his head this way and that, his eyes swept the attentive crowd, but she had seemingly vanished into thin air.

Thirteen

"Where the devil—?"

The drums began to beat again, at a much slower rhythm. Scout wasn't interested in watching another dance. He wanted to find Chantal and finish their conversation. But this celebration was being held in his honor. It would be churlish to offend his gracious hosts. So he begrudgingly returned his attention to the center of the circle, where two files of young women were moving toward him.

Their grass skirts swished around their bare legs. Their hips moved with hypnotic precision and grace. As before, the dance was sensual and seductive without being lewd.

When they reached him, the files divided, the dancers peeling off to the left and right. He was enjoying the synchronization, the spectacle, until all that remained were the last two dancers in the file. One moved away, following the others. One stayed.

He was suddenly staring into a pair of brilliant blue eyes.

His heart skipped several beats. He was spellbound by the blatant invitation in those eyes. She had removed the bikini top she had been wearing. Her breasts were bare and gleaming, inadequately veiled by a garland of plumeria. The flickering torchlight made her skin glisten. Her hair shimmied around her torso until she flung her head back. Then it swirled and swayed behind her.

In time to the evocative beat of the drums, she raised her arms above her head. They were fluid and graceful, her hands expressive. He admired her grace and skill, but he was absolutely entranced by her seductiveness. His eyes riveted on her sleek, supple belly and the undulating movements she coaxed from it. The grass skirt rippled against her thighs, giving him glimpses of smooth flesh that made his mouth water.

There was a hammering inside his head. It was louder than the volcano eruption, more powerful than the effects of the liquor. His blood grew hot and flowed thickly through his veins. It concentrated in his loins until he moaned from the delicious, stretching pressure.

With fingertips reaching heavenward, head thrown back in pagan abandon, back arched, Chantal whirled madly. On a last pounding crescendo of the drums, she collapsed in front of him, head bent low over her knees.

Then, flinging her head up, tossing her hair back like a black satin sheet, she glared at him with the fierce hunger of a woman and the proud challenge of a lioness.

Scout surged to his feet and thrust his hand down to her. She laid hers against his rough palm. He helped her up, then swept her into his arms.

Through the balmy darkness he carried her up the incline to the house. The moon was so bright, no lights were necessary. He could see his way clearly into her bedroom, though some force other than himself guided his footsteps, because his eyes never left Chantal's.

He ducked beneath the mosquito netting and laid her gently on the bed, following her down, covering her body with his. His open lips took hers in a long, delving kiss. Gently but thoroughly, his tongue plumbed her mouth while his hands stroked her body. He broke the band of the grass skirt and tossed it to the floor, leaving her in only a pair of bikini panties and a necklace of fragrant flowers.

He levered himself up so he could look at her. Her breasts lay soft and full against her chest which tapered into the flat, taut plane of her abdomen. Easing his hands into the tight fabric, he removed the bikini. Her mound was soft, dark, feathery, beautiful with mysterious promise.

He lowered his head, nudged the flowers aside, and kissed her breasts. Languorously, he dampened the centers with his tongue and felt them grow hard against it. He thrilled to the sound of her gasping his name. He wanted her to be pleased. When he slid his hand between her thighs and felt the creamy welcome of her womanhood, he knew that she was.

Quickly, he stood at the edge of the bed and began tearing at the buttons of his shirt. Chantal was released from the web of sensuality his caresses had spun around her. She sat up and reached for his hands, arresting their frantic attempts to get his clothes off.

"Let me."

"I don't know if I can wait," he said with a self-deprecating smile.

"You can."

She assumed the task of undoing the buttons, delaying completion as long as possible. When she peeled back his shirt, she pressed her open mouth against his warm, damp flesh, kissing the very center of his chest.

Groaning with pleasure, he sank his fingers into her hair. As her lips dusted kisses on his chest, she removed his shirt and dropped it to the floor. She lined her fingers up against his ribs, so that the heels of her hands met along that satiny stripe of hair that bisected his torso. She delicately tracked it with her lips.

His eyes were closed in ecstasy, his clenched teeth bared as she slowly and delicately kissed her way down. But when she began lowering his briefs, he opened his eyes and gazed down at her.

Placing a finger beneath her chin, he tilted her head up and rubbed his thumb across her moist mouth. "I don't expect anything. You don't have to do anything."

"I know. That's why I want to."

She took him, full and firm, between her hands.

"Chantal," he groaned.

She loved him with her mouth. Thoroughly. Languidly. With pleasure. Scout began to die a slow, marvelous death.

"Are you sure?"

Her hands smoothed over his buttocks and drew him closer. "*Oui.* Yes."

"Ah, that's wonderful. But I'm so deep I feel like I'm hurting you. Tell me if I hurt you."

"You won't."

Chantal closed her eyes and savored the pressure he created inside her. She welcomed his heaviness on top of her. The flowers of her lei were crushed between their bodies. Their perfume filled the sexually charged atmosphere. The feel of his chest hair against her breasts was thrilling. She loved running her hands over the hard muscles of his back, muscles she had admired when he went shirtless.

"I can't . . . can't hold back," he whispered raggedly. "Don't."

He began to move within her, stroking the walls of her body. Her hips responded to the rhythm he set and matched it. He rasped intimate, erotic words into her ear, and she spoke to him in a mindless blend of French and English. His thrusts became more powerful, creating more friction.

Chantal felt a tightening in all her muscles, a building tension that was unbearable yet blissful. His mouth found the peak of her breast, and when he tugged on it, the tension snapped. Every sensation she had ever known or imagined was funneled toward the center of her being. They exploded, giving off more light and heat than a new star. Sparks shimmered through her.

Even better, though, was feeling the burst of life from Scout's body filling hers.

"So I guess the reason I find it difficult to delegate responsibility is because I always had to assume it."

"Didn't your parents applaud your ambitions?" Cheek resting on his chest, Chantal idly strummed his nipple with her thumb.

"Sure. But they were on a fixed income. I knew if I was going to go to college and elevate myself above the factory job my father had held for thirty years, I'd have to do it on my own. They couldn't support me financially. I worked several jobs at a time to put myself through school."

"It paid off. Obviously, you've done very well."

"I got experience in several firms before going out on my own. My business started out small. That's why the Coral Reef project was such a boost. It was my first contract with a major corporation."

Mention of the Coral Reef made the outside world

seem uncomfortably near. Instinctively, she inched closer to him. He automatically closed his arms tighter around her.

"Until I came here," he said dreamily, "I thought the world revolved around the clock. I was obsessed with deadlines and schedules and the next big job." He lifted her hand to his mouth and pressed a kiss into the palm. "You've taught me that things have a way of taking care of themselves in their own good time. I haven't even missed my wristwatch."

She could feel his smile against the crown of her head. "Since I grew up in this culture, the hectic pace of life in the States frightens me. I realize that, of necessity, life there can't move as it does here, but there ought to be a happy medium," she said sadly.

"I admit that I harbored a certain amount of contempt for so-called civilization when compared to the simple life on the island," she added, "but I learned this week that this culture isn't perfect either."

"How so?"

"The business with André. I suppose every society has corruption and deceit."

"Because societies are comprised of human beings and human beings are fallible. You, for instance, have a penchant for lying."

"Oh!" She propped herself up and glared at him with mock ferocity.

Laughing, he hugged her hard. When they resettled, his wide grin faltered. He ran his knuckle down her cheek, but his touch was tentative. "I wish I knew what you were thinking, princess."

"About what?"

"About this. Us. I want you to know—"

"No." She pressed her fingertips against his lips. She didn't want anything unpleasant to spoil this time of theirs, especially their own consciences. Margot had been willing to sacrifice anything to demonstrate her love for André. Chantal believed that Margot's choice had merit.

Scout would never belong to her. He belonged to a woman she would never meet, to a society where she would no doubt be shunned. No, she wouldn't have Scout's life but, temporarily, she could have his love. While he was giving it, she was going to take it and pay the price of heartache later.

"Don't say anything, Scout. I don't want justifications or explanations. Please."

"There are things that should be said, that need to be said."

"Please," she appealed earnestly.

He sighed with resignation. "Okay, but you can't stop me from saying that you are without a doubt the finest specimen of woman I've ever seen. Your face, your body," he said hoarsely as his eyes roved down her.

"You are perfect and without equal. But it's more than just the way you look. You're exotic and rare and mysterious and intriguing and capricious and unpredictable and sexy. And even all those adjectives don't paint the full picture of Chantal Louise duPont."

He rubbed strands of her hair through his fingertips as though marveling over its silkiness. "Today, while you were overseeing preparations for the celebration, I read some of your manuscript for the textbook."

He looked at her and mused out loud, "You're brilliant, aren't you? I'm a reasonably intelligent person, but I didn't know what the hell I'd read after I'd read it. Beauty, brains, sensitivity, a real sense of self and yet concern for other people." He shrugged helplessly. "You are what every woman should aspire to be."

After a long, telling kiss, she sat up beside him and leaned back on her heels. "I don't know if I can be that poetic."

"I wasn't being poetic. Just truthful."

Lovingly, she touched his face. "I think you're very handsome."

"Thanks."

"I mean it. When you were pointed out to me at the gala, my heart fluttered. I was glad it was you I had to entice." She drew her finger around his stern chin. "You're stubborn. You get impatient with yourself too easily. But I admire a strong will. You're insightful and never turn your back on a problem or responsibility. You're sensitive to and respectful of other people's feelings." Her fingertips plowed through his chest hair and lightly coasted down his torso. "I like your hairy chest. It's very sexy."

He growled. "I love being adored." Feeling cocky, he stacked his hands behind his head. "Tell me more."

"I was just about to comment on how prominent your ribs are," she said impishly, and laughed when his complacent smile collapsed. "You're thinner than when you arrived."

"No wonder, with the healthy diet I've been on and how many calories I sweat off every day."

Her fingers trailed over his abdomen to his thighs. She gently touched the fresh scar. "I'm very, very sorry."

"I know."

"I couldn't believe it when the gun went off in my hand and I saw your blood. I swear I didn't mean to shoot you. I didn't—"

He squeezed her hand. "I *know*."

She lifted his hand and curved it around her throat.

"You were so angry when you regained consciousness and realized what had happened."

"Yeah, I was. But . . ." His eyes moved over her
with rekindled desire. "More painful than the gunshot was how badly I wanted you. I feel like I was
born hard from wanting you." He pulled her down to
his level. Several exploratory kisses later, he murmured against her lips, "I want to touch you."

"Like this?" She moved his hand down to her
breast. He enfolded it. Sitting up, he took the stiff
nipple between his lips and tantalized it before drawing it into his mouth.

"Scout," she cried breathlessly.

"I want to be inside you."

Within seconds he was, and she was moving above
him. He slid his hands over her breasts and down
her torso until his fingertips played in the delta of
soft hair. He slipped his hand between their bodies
and intimately caressed her with the pads of his
fingers, while watching her face grow flushed with
passion.

Her breathing was rough. Sensations washed over
her like warm, breaking waves. She drowned in them.
As they climaxed simultaneously, her soul cried out,
"I love you," though she was never certain if the
words actually left her lips.

Afterward, she fell forward upon his chest, too
exhausted and sated even to move from him.

Smoothing his hands over her dewy skin, he whispered, "You said that the soul of the volcano was
inside your father. It lives inside you too, Chantal. I
can feel it pulsing around me, like a heartbeat."

It was day and he was leaving.

She wasn't surprised. She had known he would.
She pretended to be asleep when he disentangled

his limbs from hers, unsnared his fingers from her hair, and left the bed. He silently collected his clothing and crept from the room.

Eyes closed, she lay unmoving, listening to the sounds of his packing. His footsteps reentered the hall. Though she kept her eyes resolutely closed, she knew the instant his silhouette filled the doorway of her bedroom and his shadow stretched across the floor.

And she knew the instant he mentally bade his island girl good-bye because a great emptiness opened up inside her, a yawning chasm that would never be filled.

Without making a sound, he left the house, never seeing the tears rolling down her cheeks onto the pillow they had shared.

Fourteen

It was cold in Boston. He'd almost forgotten what cold, damp weather felt like, how it chilled to the marrow. The heater in Jennifer's BMW was going full blast. So were her vocal cords. She hadn't stopped talking since she had picked him up at the airport.

"I really should be furious with you." Adroitly, she swerved to miss a taxicab on the entrance ramp of the highway. "When you called me from California I almost hung up on you before you could explain where you had been and why."

She had been waiting at the curb outside the terminal and had gaily tooted her horn and waved at him as he emerged, carrying his one suitcase and shivering in his insufficient clothing. As he stashed his suitcase in the backseat, she had apologized for not meeting him at the gate.

"But that would have entailed parking and walking all the way through the airport and, well, it just wasn't necessary," she had said, leaning over and proffering her lips, which he had perfunctorily kissed.

Now she reached across the console and tentatively patted his thigh. "I can't believe you were shot by a native! My God, Scout, it must have been just awful. You'll have to tell me all about it. But first I want to fill you in on everything that's been going on while you were away."

She launched into a litany of births and breakups that had occurred among her circle of friends and acquaintances. "Before I forget, Mr. Reynolds—although he insists I start calling him Corey—called yesterday. When I told him you were on your way home, he invited us to have dinner with him and Mrs. Reynolds tomorrow night. I accepted." Her voice dropped to a confidential whisper. "I think he wants to make you an offer you can't refuse. Isn't that exciting?"

Had she always been this talkative?

"Mother was so stressed out because she was afraid you weren't going to make it back in time for the wedding, she had to go to bed and was put on medication. When you called, she had a miraculous recovery and started referring to you as 'that poor dear.' So you're forgiven for being detained. Yesterday, arrangements for the wedding got back into full swing."

Wedding. Marriage. Scout looked at the woman who was combating Boston traffic for him and wondered why he'd ever asked her to marry him. She was pretty, educated, cultured. After devoting himself almost exclusively to building his business and seeing the ripe age of forty rushing toward him, he had started giving some thought to his personal life.

He wanted a family. He wanted kids. Jennifer had come along about that time. She had been marriage material: bright, articulate, and presentable to potential clients. He hadn't been involved with anyone else at the time, so . . .

"Daddy says Hawaii, but Mother says Hawaii is so blasé. *Everybody* goes to Hawaii to honeymoon. Besides, I said that you were probably sick of tropical climes, so I suggested they send us to Spain or North Africa, something different. I don't know anybody who's been to North Africa on their honeymoon. Wait and see, we'll start a trend."

He gazed out the rain-splattered windshield. The soft floral-scented breeze, the sound of the surf, the call of jungle birds, seemed light-years away. He was already homesick for them and had been away for only three days. Four? How long had he been on an airplane?

"Darling, you look positively exhausted," Jennifer commented, catching him wearily rubbing his temples. "I'm taking you to my place for tonight because I'm sure your apartment needs to be cleaned and aired before it's fit for human occupancy. I'm sending my maid over there tomorrow.

"Tonight I want you to relax, first by taking a long, hot shower. And please shave. I've never seen you looking so scruffy. In the morning you can make an emergency appointment with your barber. Thank heaven I planned to have dinner in tonight. You'd frighten any respectable maître d' in town."

She parked at the curb in front of her town house and cut the motor. "Tomorrow you can start—"

"Jennifer."

She looked at him with surprise. "My goodness, do you realize that's the first thing you've said since you got in the car? Don't worry about it." She laid a consoling hand on his arm. "After all the traveling you've done, you're entitled to be a little moody. You'll feel better once we get inside. I've got a fire burning in the den and margaritas in the fridge. Dinner's ready to go into the oven. I'll put it in at seven, so we can eat no later than eight. Please make sure you've showered and shaved before then."

She was a lovely young woman, who would make

an upwardly mobile man a perfect wife. He had thought she was everything he wanted. Efficient. Organized. Bubbly. Maybe that was it. She was just too . . . bubbly.

"Jennifer, I'll call Corey Reynolds myself and cancel our dinner date." Her lips parted in stunned surprise, but he continued before she could interrupt. "I need to discuss business with him, but I'd rather keep the meeting strictly business."

"I don't understand why, but if that's the way you want it, all right." Her mouth pursed petulantly. She hated for carefully laid plans to go awry.

"And you cancel the wedding."

He hadn't planned to break it to her so soon. He had planned to ease into it. But he saw no reason to delay the inevitable. It wasn't fair to her, and he couldn't bear the strain a second longer.

He was amazed how quickly the tension in his chest began to subside. It was like the stitches of a garment that was too tight suddenly popping free. After those first words were out, the rest were easy.

"I realize this is a hideous thing to do. Call me a bastard and you'll be right. But not as bad a bastard as I'd be if I went through with this marriage. You see"—he paused and drew a deep breath—"I don't love you. I love somebody else. Very much."

"Gone?" Scout repeated. "Gone? Gone where? To the other side of the island? Swimming? Fishing? To Voix de Tonnerre? Where?"

It had taken him a month, one long month, to return the hundreds of messages his answering service had been saving, sort through and respond to his mail, pay all his bills, and make necessary business contacts.

Corey Reynolds had been disappointed that Scout

was no longer engaged to the charming Jennifer, but he offered Scout three very lucrative contract jobs that would keep him busy for the next two years. Before his signature on the dotted line had time to dry, Scout informed Corey that before he began the first project he had some personal business to attend to, then hopped the next plane to Honolulu.

Upon finally reaching Parrish Island, he rented a jeep and struck out for the village. He had difficulty finding his way along the winding, mountainous roads and ran into one dead end after another.

He began to believe that the village and Chantal were all a long dream from which he hadn't yet awakened. But keeping the volcano at his right, he eventually came to the ravine. The thatched roofs on the other side testified that it was real and not a figment of his imagination.

He honked the horn of the jeep and shouted, waving his arms over his head like a flagman on an aircraft carrier. Several villagers who spotted him first ran to alert the others.

He didn't see Chantal yet, but he scrambled down the steps he had so recently installed, ran across the bridge, then up the steps of the other side. He was breathless when he reached the summit. Johnny hurled himself against Scout's legs and hugged them hard.

André approached, a smiling Margot at his side. After the initial greetings, Scout's eyes eagerly scanned the crowd of faces but didn't see the one he most hungered to see. When he asked for Chantal, André answered him with a phrase that echoed like a death knell inside his skull.

"Gone to America."

"America?" Scout wheezed. "When?"

"Weeks ago."

"Why?"

André seemed at a loss. Scout elbowed people aside on his rush toward her house. He ran up the path and across the veranda. "Chantal!" he shouted as he flung open the door.

Only silence greeted him. The furniture was still intact, but all personal items had been removed. No more books. No more photographs. He ran through the house like a madman, throwing open closet doors and drawers, but it became apparent that she was gone.

More slowly, he walked through the house. He noticed that her mother's dressing table was missing. With a detached, rational part of his mind, he calculated how difficult it must have been to get across the ravine. She must have wanted it very badly. That she had taken it indicated she wasn't coming back.

He sat down on the edge of the bed they had shared only once and plowed his fingers through his hair, hanging his head between his hands, a living definition of despair.

"Miss duPont," he said with succinct impatience. "Is she on the faculty or not?"

Once he had returned to the States, he had begun his search at UCLA. The secretary at the administration office of the earth science college gave him a condescending once-over. "Sir, are you referring to Dr. duPont?"

"Dr. duPont? Yes, yes. Chantal duPont."

He was given terse directions to her office building. He raced there in his rented car, parked illegally, and ran inside. After consulting the register, he took the elevator to the third floor and jogged along the hallway, counting down the numbers stenciled on the doors. When he reached hers, he firmly twisted the brass doorknob and shoved open the door.

She was standing at a wide window with her back to him. It looked odd to see her dressed in a tailored suit. Her hair was pulled back into a neat bun on her nape.

"Chantal!"

She turned. He was looking into the face of a total stranger.

Epilogue

Her spectacular view of the Pacific sunset was suddenly blocked by a pair of trousers, rolled up at the cuffs, and bare feet. She angled her head back and shaded her eyes against the sun, which was just about to be swallowed by the horizon.

"Scout!" The name that was never far from her mind rushed past her lips on a breathless whisper.

"I'm flattered. You remember."

He dropped to his knees in the sand. His brows were drawn within touching distance of each other, forming a scowl that was achingly familiar and endearing.

"What are you doing here?"

"What do you think? Looking for you. Why did you leave?"

"The island?" Somewhat confused, she shook her head slightly. "I always planned to when Father died. There were only two things I had to do first. Finish his last book and—"

"Build the bridge."

"That was Father's last wish. He wanted it to be his legacy to the people of the village. When it was completed, there was nothing to hold me there."

"I thought the island was home to you."

She gazed reflectively into the surf. "It was different for me there than it was for my father. He had Mother and me. His life there was complete. I, on the other hand, have no family. There was important work waiting for me here." Her eyes moved back to Scout. She lifted her shoulders in an expressive shrug.

Scout was far from mollified. "Do you know the hell I've gone through to find you? I flew back to Parrish, drove miles through that infernal jungle, battled the heat, the insects, everything, only to discover when I got there that you were gone."

He took a breath. "Today I went straight from the airport to the university and turned the place upside down. I got to your office and scared the living daylights out of your assistant. She had her hair—oh, never mind. That part isn't important.

"I tried convincing her that I wasn't a maniac, but she called to confirm it was all right to give me your address. I made her let the phone ring at least a hundred times. I guess you were out here."

"I sit on the beach most evenings and watch the sunset."

He glanced up at her house, a small, neat structure perched on the cliff above them, overlooking the beach. "It's nice here. Reminiscent of the island."

"That's why I bought it. Go on with your story."

"I threatened your assistant with bodily harm if she didn't give me your address. After one and a half death-defying hours on the freeway and two wrong turns, I finally made it."

"You went to all that trouble to find me? Why?"

"Why did you sleep with me?" he asked pointedly.

In his present mood she didn't think it would be prudent to be either glib or evasive. His frown demanded candor. "Because I love you." He looked skeptical. That touched her as nothing else had. She reached for his hand and pressed it. "This isn't one of my tricks, one of my white lies. I give you my word about this. I knew I loved you the night we went to Voix de Tonnerre."

It was a while before he spoke. "Why didn't you tell me then?"

"Because I knew you would leave me anyway."

"And you didn't want me to feel bound."

"That's right."

"I had to leave when I did, Chantal," he said, reversing their hands so that he was now clasping hers. "I tried to explain the night before, but you wouldn't let me, remember? You thought I regarded you as an island girl, an object to amuse myself with until I returned home. Believing that, you still made love to me?"

Unable to speak, she nodded.

"What that must have cost you," he said on a rush of air. Reaching out, he cupped her face in his palms. She felt the calluses against her cheeks. "Listen to me. Jennifer is a thing of the past. I broke our engagement."

"Oh, how horrible."

"It was, yes. I couldn't continue making love to you while she was still officially in the picture, so for the sake of time I had to be blunt."

"What did she say?"

"Lots of things. But it wasn't so much what she said as what she didn't say. She went on at great length about inconvenience and embarrassment, but she didn't once tell me that she loved me deeply and that I'd broken her heart.

"Look," he said earnestly, "I'm not proud of treating her the way I did. But we would never have made it. In a few years, if that long, we would have been going through a divorce. All her friends get divorces. It's fashionable. I was handy to her, just as she was to me, at a point when both of us figured it was time to get married. So don't feel guilty about ruining a grand love affair. It never was. If it had been, I wouldn't have followed you from that ballroom."

Chantal wanted to be convinced. "She seemed so right for you."

"Yes, she did, but I wasn't in love with her. I fell in love with you. Wrong place. Wrong time. Wrong everything. But you are the woman I love." He tilted her face up and kissed her extraordinary cheekbone.

"You love me?"

"Can you doubt it?"

Her heart brimmed with love and joy, but she was still unsure of his plans for the future. Much as she loved him, she wouldn't be his mistress, an exotic plaything, a novelty. "What's going to happen?"

"You're going to marry me, princess. And we're going to have babies, because I can't think of anything more rewarding than mixing my genes with yours."

Her radiant smile lasted for only several seconds before dimming. "But what about your work? Mine? Where will we live?"

"We'll work it out," he vowed softly. "If we love each other enough, we'll manage to merge our lives successfully."

Her eyes were shimmering with tears. After weeks of thinking that she would never see him again, she couldn't believe that he was kneeling in front of her, professing a love that obviously equaled hers for him. She touched his hair, his brows, his shoulders, as if to reassure herself that she wasn't having a vivid fantasy.

"I'll want to go back to the island periodically."

"Once a year," he said, apparently having already given it some thought. "We'll stay a month. It'll be our annual family vacation. We'll let the kids run naked on the beach, absorb a different culture, observe the volcano, learn about their French grandfather and Polynesian grandmother. Besides, I promised Johnny."

"Scout," she whispered, laying her hands against his lean cheeks, "can it work?"

"Do you love me?"

"With my whole being."

"Then it'll work." His kiss conveyed as much confidence as his words. It was a hungry, searching kiss that left them weak with desire.

Her hair was already hanging loose. He combed his fingers through it, then unbuttoned the shirt she was wearing and took it off. The brassiere surprised him. He'd never known her to wear one.

"Civilization," she said softly.

"To hell with that."

When her breasts were exposed to the lavender sky, the sand, the salt spray, and his lips, he eased her back onto the sand. Moments later he stretched out naked beside her and pulled her into his arms. "I love all the women you are, but I think you're most beautiful just as you are now, natural and uninhibited."

He removed her shorts, knelt between her thighs, and sweetly kissed her navel, then nuzzled her cleft. "You know," he said emotionally as he angled himself above her, "for all the time I spent in paradise, I never once made love on the beach."

She curled her hand around the back of his neck and drew him down, whispering, "Neither did I."

THE EDITOR'S CORNER

What an extraordinary sextet of heroes we have for you next month! And the heroines are wonderful, too, but who's paying all that much attention when there are such fantastic men around?

Iris Johansen is back with a vibrantly emotional, truly thrilling romance, **MAGNIFICENT FOLLY**, LOVESWEPT #342. Iris's man of the month is Andrew Ramsey. (Remember him? Surprised to reencounter him as a hero? Well, he is a marvelous—no, magnificent—one!) When this handsome, unusually talented, and sensitive man appears in Lily Deslin's life, she almost goes into shock. The intuitive stranger attracts her wildly, while almost scaring her to death. Abruptly, Lily learns that Andrew has played a very special, very intimate role in her life and, having appeared as if by magic, is on the scene to protect her and her beloved daughter Cassie. Before the danger from the outside world begins, Lily is already in trouble because Andrew is unleashing in her powerful emotions and a deep secret she's kept buried for years. Iris's **GOLDEN CLASSIC, THE TRUSTWORTHY RED-HEAD,** is now on sale. If you read it—and we hope you will—we believe you'll have an especially wonderful time with **MAGNIFICENT FOLLY,** as Andrew, Lily, and Cassie take you back to Alex Ben Rashid's Sedikhan.

Ivan Rasmussen is one of the most gorgeous and dashing heroes ever . . . and you won't want to miss his love story in Janet Evanovich's **IVAN TAKES A WIFE**, LOVESWEPT #343. The fun begins when Stephanie Lowe substitutes for her cousin as cook on board Ivan's windjammer cruise in Maine coastal waters. Descended from a pirate, Ivan sweeps Stephanie off her feet while laughing at her Calamity Jane performance in his galley. He had never thought of settling down until he embraced Stephanie, and she had never been made to feel cherished until Ivan teased and flirted with her. But Stephanie has her hands full—a house that's falling apart, a shrivelling bank account, and some *very* strange goings-on that keep her and Ivan jumping once they're back on terra firma. There is a teenager in this story who is an absolutely priceless character as far as those of us on the LOVESWEPT staff are concerned. We hope you enjoy

(continued)

her and her remarkable role in this affair as much as we did. Full of humor and passion, **IVAN TAKES A WIFE** is a real winner!

Imagine meeting a red-bearded giant of a man who has muscles like boulders and a touch as gentle as rose petals. If you can dream him up, then you have a fair picture of Joker Vandergriff, Sandra Chastain's hero in **JOKER'S WILD**, LOVESWEPT #344. We can only thank Sandra for taking us in this story back to delightful Lizard Rock, with its magical hot springs and its wonderful people, where Joker is determined to heal the injuries of former Olympic skater Allison Josey. He mesmerizes her into accepting his massages, his tender touches, his sweet concern . . . his scorching kisses. Her wounds are emotional as well as physical, and they run deep. Joker has to fight her demons with all his considerable power. Then, in a dramatic twist, the tables turn and Joker has to learn to accept Allison's gift of love. As heartwarming as it is exciting, **JOKER'S WILD** leaves you feeling that all is more than right with the world.

Rugged, virile, smart, good-looking—that's Nick Jordan, hero of the intense and warm romance **TIGRESS**, LOVESWEPT #345, by Charlotte Hughes. What a dreamboat this sexy peach farmer is . . . and what a steamy delight is his romance with Natalie Courtland, a woman he finds stranded on his property during a freak snowstorm. The cabin fever they come to share has nothing to do with going stir-crazy as the storm keeps them confined to his home; it has everything to do with the wild attraction between them. Beyond their desire for each other, though, they seem to have nothing in common. Natalie is a divorce lawyer in Atlanta, and Nick has forsaken the world of glamorous condos, designer clothes, sophisticated entertainment, for a way of life he considers more real, more meaningful. How they resolve their differences so that love triumphs will keep you on the edge of your chair. A true delight first to last!

Ooh, la, la, here comes Mr. Tall, Dark, and Handsome himself—Dutton McHugh, Joan Elliott Pickart's devastating hero of **SWEET BLISS**, LOVESWEPT #346. When Bliss Barton wakes up with her first ever hangover, she finds a half-naked hunk in her bed! She could die of

(continued)

mortification—especially when she recognizes him as one of her brother's rowdy buddies. Dutton is not her type at all. Careful, cautious, an outsider in her family of free spirits, Bliss has kept her wild oats tightly packed away—while Dutton has scattered his to the four winds. When her family misunderstands the relationship between Bliss and Dutton, and applauds what they imagine is going on, Bliss decides to make it real. The hilarious and touching romance that follows is a true joy to read!

Fayrene Preston outdoes herself in creating her hero in **AMETHYST MIST,** LOVESWEPT #347. Brady McCullough is the epitome of rugged masculinity, sex appeal, and mystery. When Marissa Berryman literally falls into his life, he undergoes a sudden and dramatic change. He is wild to possess her . . . not just for a night, but for all time. The confirmed bachelor, the ultimate loner has met his fate. And Marissa, who goes up in flames at his touch, is sure she's found her home at last. Parted by the legacies of their pasts, they have to make great personal journeys of understanding and change to fulfill their destiny to love. A breathlessly exciting love story with all of Fayrene's wonderfully evocative writing in full evidence!

I reminded you about Iris's **GOLDEN CLASSIC,** but don't forget the three other marvelous reissues now on sale . . . **SOMETHING DIFFERENT,** by Kay Hooper; **THAT OLD FEELING,** by Fayrene Preston; and **TEMPORARY ANGEL,** by Billie Green. What fabulous romance reading. Enjoy!

With every good wish,

Carolyn Nichols

Carolyn Nichols
Editor
LOVESWEPT
Bantam Books
666 Fifth Avenue
New York, NY 10103

THE DELANEY DYNASTY

Men and women whose loves and passions are so glorious it takes many great romance novels by three bestselling authors to tell their tempestuous stories.

THE SHAMROCK TRINITY

☐ 21975 **RAFE, THE MAVERICK**
    by Kay Hooper $2.95

☐ 21976 **YORK, THE RENEGADE**
    by Iris Johansen $2.95

☐ 21977 **BURKE, THE KINGPIN**
    by Fayrene Preston $2.95

THE DELANEYS OF KILLAROO

☐ 21872 **ADELAIDE, THE ENCHANTRESS**
    by Kay Hooper $2.75

☐ 21873 **MATILDA, THE ADVENTURESS**
    by Iris Johansen $2.75

☐ 21874 **SYDNEY, THE TEMPTRESS**
    by Fayrene Preston $2.75

☐ 26991 **THIS FIERCE SPLENDOR**
    by Iris Johansen $3.95

Now Available!
THE DELANEYS: *The Untamed Years*

☐ 21897 **GOLDEN FLAMES** *by Kay Hooper* $3.50
☐ 21898 **WILD SILVER** *by Iris Johansen* $3.50
☐ 21999 **COPPER FIRE** *by Fayrene Preston* $3.50

Buy these books at your local bookstore or use this page to order.

Prices and availability subject to change without notice.

- -

Bantam Books, Dept. SW7, 414 East Golf Road, Des Plaines, IL 60016

Please send me the books I have checked above. I am enclosing $_____ (please add $2.00 to cover postage and handling). Send check or money order—no cash or C.O.D.s please.

Mr/Ms _____

Address _____

City/State _____ Zip _____

                                    SW7—4/89
Please allow four to six weeks for delivery. This offer expires 10/89.

BANTAM
SHOP-AT-HOME
C·A·T·A·L·O·G

Special Offer
Buy a Bantam Book
for only 50¢.

Now you can have Bantam's catalog filled with hundreds of titles plus take advantage of our unique and exciting bonus book offer. A special offer which gives you the opportunity to purchase a Bantam book for only 50¢. Here's how!

By ordering any five books at the regular price per order, you can also choose any other single book listed (up to a $5.95 value) for just 50¢. Some restrictions do apply, but for further details why not send for Bantam's catalog of titles today!

Just send us your name and address and we will send you a catalog!

BANTAM BOOKS, INC.
P.O. Box 1006, South Holland, Ill. 60473

Mr./Mrs./Ms. _____
(please print)

Address _____

City _____ State _____ Zip _____
FC(A)—10/87
Please allow four to six weeks for delivery.